CHRISTIE'S OLD ORGAN

CHRISTIE'S OLD ORGAN

by
Mrs. O. F. WALTON

LUTTERWORTH PRESS
CAMBRIDGE

Lutterworth Press
P.O. Box 60
Cambridge CB1 2NT

ALL RIGHTS RESERVED
New Edition 1948
Reprinted 1949, 1955, 1959,
1962, 1966, 1972, 1976, 1977
First paperback edition 1989

British Library Cataloguing in Publication Data
Walton, O. F.
  Christie's old organ.
  I. Title
  823′.912 [J]
  ISBN 0-7188-2804 6

Printed and bound in Great Britain by
The Guernsey Press Co. Ltd., Guernsey, Channel Islands

Contents

1
The Old Organ

"HOME, sweet home, there's no place like home, there's no place like home," played the unmusical notes of a barrel-organ in the top room of a lodging-house in a dreary back street. The words certainly did not seem to apply to that dismal abode; there were not many there who knew much of the sweets of home.

It was a very dark, uncomfortable place, and as the lodgers in the lower room turned over on their wretched beds, many of which were merely bare wooden benches, it may be that one and another gave a sigh as he thought how far he was from "Home, sweet home".

But the organ played on, though the hour was late, and the dip candle was put out, and the fire was dying away. If you had climbed the crooked staircase, you would have seen an old man sitting alone in his attic, and smiling at his organ as he turned it with a trembling hand.

Old Treffy loved his barrel-organ; it was the one comfort of his life. He was a poor, forlorn old man, without a friend in the world. Every one that he had ever loved was dead; he had no one to whom he could talk, or to whom he could tell his troubles. And thus he gathered up all the remaining bits and fragments of love in his old heart, faded and withered though they were, and he gave them all to his old organ, which had well-nigh seen as many summers as he had. It was getting very antiquated and old-fashioned now; the red silk in front of it was very soiled and worn, and it could not play any of the new tunes of which the children were so fond. It sometimes struck old Treffy that he and his organ were very much alike - they were getting altogether behind the age; and people looked down on them and pushed past them, as they hurried along the street. And though old Treffy was very patient, yet he could not help feeling this.

He had felt it very much on the day of which I am writing. It was cold, dismal weather; a cutting east wind had swept round the corners of the streets, and had chilled the old man through and through. His threadbare coat could not keep it out; how could he expect it to do so, when he had worn it so many years he could scarcely count them? His thin, trembling old hands were so benumbed with cold that he could scarcely feel the handle of the organ, and, as he turned it, he made sundry little shakes and quavers in the tune, which were certainly not intended by the maker of the old barrel-organ.

There was not much variety in the tunes old Treffy could play. There was the *Old Hundredth*, and *Poor Mary Ann*, and *Rule Britannia*; the only other one was *Home, sweet Home*, but that was old Treffy's favourite. He always played it very slowly, to make it last longer, and on this cold day the shakes and quavers in it sounded most pathetic.

But no one took much notice of old Treffy or his organ. A little crowd of children gathered round him, and asked him for all sorts of new tunes of which he had never even heard the names.

They did not seem to care for *Home, sweet Home*, or the *Old Hundredth*, and soon moved away. Then an old gentleman put his head out of a window, and in a cross voice told him to move on, and not disturb a quiet neighbourhood with his noise. Old Treffy meekly obeyed, and, battling with the rough east wind, he tried another and a more bustling street; but here a policeman warned him to depart, lest he should crowd up the way.

Poor old Treffy, was almost fainting, but he must not give up, for he had not a halfpenny in his pocket, and he had come out without breakfast. At length a kind-hearted farmer's wife, who was passing with a basket on her arm, took pity on the old man, and gave him a penny from her capacious pocket.

Thus all day long Treffy played on; over and over again his four tunes were sounded forth, but that was the only penny he received that cold day.

At last, as the daylight was fading, he turned homeward. On his way he parted with his solitary penny for a cake of bread, and slowly and wearily he dragged himself up the steep stairs to his lonely attic.

Poor old Treffy was in bad spirits this evening. He felt that he and his organ were getting out of date, things of the past. They were growing old together. He could remember the day when it was new. How proud he had been of it! Oh, how he had admired it! The red silk was quite bright, and the tunes were all the fashion. There were not so many organs about then, and people stopped to listen - not children only, but grown men and women - and Treffy had been a proud man in those days. But a generation had grown up since then, and now Treffy felt that he was a poor, lone old man, very far behind the age, and that his organ was getting too old-fashioned for the present day. He felt very cast down and dismal, as he raked together the cinders, and tried to make a little blaze in the small fire he had lit.

But when he had eaten his cake, and had taken some tea which he had warmed over again, old Treffy felt rather better, and he turned as usual to his old organ to cheer his fainting spirits. For old Treffy knew nothing of a better Comforter.

The landlady of the house had objected at first to old Treffy's organ; she said it disturbed the lodgers; but on Treffy's offering to pay a penny a week extra for his little attic, on condition of his being able to play whenever he liked, she made no further opposition.

And thus, till late in the night, he turned away, and his face grew brighter and his heart lighter, as he listened to his four tunes. It was such good company, he said, and the attic was so lonely at night. And there was no one to find fault with the organ there, or to call it old-fashioned. Treffy admired it with all his heart, and felt that at night at least it had justice done to it.

But there was one who was listening to the old organ, and admiring it as much as old Treffy, of whom the old man knew nothing. Outside the door, crouching down with his ear against a large crack, lay a little ragged boy; he had come into the lodging-room downstairs to sleep, and had lain down on one of the hard benches, when old Treffy's barrel-organ began to play. He had not listened to it much at first, but when the first notes of *Home, sweet Home*, had been sounded forth, little Christie had raised his head on his elbow, and listened with all his might. It was almost too much for him; it was a memory of the past. A few months ago, little Christie had a mother, and this was the last tune she sang. It brought it all back to him: the bare, desolate room, the wasted form on the bed, the dear, loving hand which had stroked his face so gently, and the sweet voice which had sung that very tune to him. He could hear her, even now: "Home, sweet home, there's no place like home; there's no place like home." How sweetly she had sung it! - he remembered it so well. And he remembered what she had said to him just afterwards -

"I'm going home, Christie - going home - home, sweet home; I'm going home, Christie."

And those were the last words she had said to him.

Since then, life had been very dreary to little Christopher. Life without a mother, it hardly *was* life to him. He had never been happy since she had died. He had worked very hard, poor little fellow, to earn his bread, for she had told him to do that. But he had often wished he could go to his mother in *Home, sweet Home*. And he wished it more than ever this night, as he heard his mother's tune. He waited very patiently for it, whilst old Treffy was playing the other three which came first, but at length someone closed the door, and the noise inside the lodging-room was so great that he could not distinguish the notes of the longed-for tune.

So Christie crept out quietly in the darkness, and closing the door softly, that no one might notice it, he stole gently upstairs.

He knelt down by the door and listened. It was very cold, and the wind swept up the staircase, and made little Christie shiver. Yet still he knelt by the door.

At length the organ stopped; he heard the old man putting it down by the wall, and in a few minutes all was still.

Then Christie crept downstairs again, and lay down once more on his hard bench, and he fell asleep, and dreamt of the mother in the far-off land. And he thought he heard her singing *"Home, sweet Home,* I'm home now, Christie; I'm home now, and there's no place like home."

2
Christie's Important Charge

THE dismal lodging-house had a charm for little Christie now. Night after night he returned there, that he might hear his mother's tune. The landlady began to look upon him as one of her regular household. She sometimes gave him a crust of bread, for she noticed his hungry face each night, as he came to the large lodging-room to sleep.

And every night old Treffy played, and Christie crept upstairs to listen.

But one night, as he was kneeling at the attic door, the music suddenly ceased, and Christie heard a dull, heavy sound, as if something had fallen on the floor. He waited a minute, but all was quite still; so he cautiously lifted the latch and peeped into the room. There was only a dim light in the attic, for the fire was nearly out, and old Treffy had no candle. But the moonlight, streaming in at the window, showed Christie the form of the old man stretched on the ground, and his poor old barrel-organ laid beside him. Christie crept to his side, and took hold of his hand. It was deadly cold, and Christie thought he was dead. He was just going to call the landlady, when the old man moved, and in a trembling voice asked, "What's the matter, and who's there?"

"It's only me, Master Treffy," said Christie, "it's only me. I was listening to your organ, I was, and I heard you tumble, so I came in. Are you better, Master Treffy?"

The old man raised his head, and looked round. Christie helped him to get up, and took him to his little straw bed in the corner of the attic.

"Are you better, Master Treffy?" he asked again.

"Yes, yes," said the old man; "it's only the cold, boy; it's very

12

chilly o' nights now, and I'm a poor lone old man. Good night."

And so the old man fell asleep, and Christie lay down by his side and slept also.

That was the beginning of a friendship between old Treffy and Christie. They were both alone in the world, both friendless and desolate, and it drew them to each other. Christie was a great comfort to Treffy. He went on errands for him, he cleaned the old attic, and he carried the barrel-organ downstairs each morning when Treffy went on his rounds. And in return, Treffy gave Christie a corner of the attic to sleep in, and let him sit over his tiny fire whilst he played his dear old organ. And whenever he came to *Home, sweet Home*, Christie thought of his mother, and of what she had said to him before she died.

"Where is 'Home sweet Home', Master Treffy?" he asked one night.

Treffy looked round the wretched little attic, with its damp, weatherstained roof, and its rickety, rotten floor, and felt that he could not call *it* "Home, sweet Home".

"It's not here, Christie," he said.

"No," said Christie, thoughtfully; "I expect it's a long way from here, Master Treffy."

"Yes," said the old man; "there must be something better somewhere."

"My mother used to talk about heaven," said Christie doubtfully. "I wonder if that was the home she meant?"

But old Treffy knew very little of heaven; no one had ever told him of the home above. Yet he thought of Christie's words many times that day, as he dragged himself about wearily, with his old organ. He was failing very fast, poor old man; his legs were becoming feeble, and he was almost fainting when he reached the attic. The cold wind had chilled him through and through.

Christie was at home before him, and had lit the fire, and boiled the kettle, and put all ready for old Treffy's comfort. He wondered what was the matter with Treffy that night; he was so quiet and silent, and he never even asked for his old organ after tea, but went to bed as soon as possible.

And the next day he was too weak and feeble to go out; and Christie watched beside him, and got him all he wanted, as tenderly as any woman could have done.

And the next day it was the same, and the day after that, till the attic cupboard grew empty, and all poor old Treffy's pence were gone.

"What are we going to do now, Christie?" he said pitifully; "I can't go out to-day, my lad, can I?"

"No," said Christie, "you mustn't think of it, Master Treffy. Let me see, what can we do? Shall *I* take the organ out?"

Old Treffy did not answer; a great struggle was going on in his mind. Could he let anyone but himself touch his dear old organ? It would be hard to see it go out, and have to stay behind - very hard indeed. But Christie was a careful lad; he would rather trust it with him than with anyone else; and he had come to his last piece of money. He must not sit still and starve. Yes, the organ must go; but it would be a great trial to him. He would be so lonely in the dark attic when Christie and the organ were both gone. What a long, tedious day it would be for him.

"Yes, Christie, you may take her to-morrow," he said at length; "but you must be *very* careful of her, my lad - *very* careful."

"All right, Master Treffy," said Christie, cheerily; "I'll bring her safe home, you see if I don't."

What a day that was in Christie's life! He was up with the lark, as people say, but there was no lark within many a mile of that dismal street. He was certainly up before the sparrows, and long before the men on the benches in the great lodging-room. He crept out cautiously into the court in the grey morning light, and kneeling by the common pump, he splashed the water upon his face and neck till they lost all feeling with the cold. Then he rubbed his hands till they were as red as cherries, and he was obliged to wrap them up in his ragged coat, that he might feel they still belonged to him. And then he stole upstairs again, and lifting the latch of the attic door very gently, lest old Treffy should awake, he combed his rough hair with a broken comb, and arranged his ragged garments to the best possible advantage.

Then Christie was ready; and he longed for the time when Old Treffy would wake, and give him leave to go. The sparrows were chirping on the eaves now, and the sun was beginning to shine. There were noises in the house, too, and one by one the men in the great lodging-room shook themselves, and went out to their work and to their labour until the evening.

Christie watched them crossing the court, and his impatience to be off grew stronger. At length he touched old Treffy's hand very gently, and the old man said, in a bewildered voice, "What is it, Christie, boy; what is it?"

"It's morning, Master Treffy," said Christie; "shall you soon be awake?"

The old man turned over in bed, and finally sat up.

"Why, Christie, boy, how nice you look!" said Treffy, admiringly.

Christie drew himself up with considerable importance, and walked up and down the attic, that Treffy might further admire him.

"Yes, Christie, boy, go if you like," said the old man; "but you'll be very careful of her, won't you, Christie?"

"Yes, Master Treffy," said the boy, "I'll be as careful as you are."

"And you'll not turn her round too fast, Christie?" he went on.

"No, Master Treffy," said Christie; "I'll turn her no faster than you do."

"And you mustn't stop and talk to boys in the street, Christie; they are very rude sometimes, are boys, and they always want the new tunes, Christie; but never you heed them. Her tunes are getting old-fashioned, poor old thing; she's something like me.

But you mustn't take no notice of the boys, Christie."

"No, Master Treffy," said Christie; "no more than you do."

"There's one tune they're very fond of," said old Treffy, meditatively; "I don't rightly know what it is 'Marshall Lazy' (*Marseillaise*) or something of that sort. I reckon it's called after some man in the wars maybe."

"You don't know who he was? asked Christie.

"No," said old Treffy, "I don't bother my head about it. I expect he was some lazy scoundrel who wouldn't do his duty, and so they made up a song to mock at him. But that's as it may be, Christie; I don't know, I'm sure. I expect he wasn't born when my organ was made; I expect not, Christie."

"Well, Master Treffy, I'm ready," said Christie, putting the organ strap over his neck; "good-bye."

And, with an air of great importance, Christie carefully descended the rickety stairs, and marched triumphantly across the court. A few children who were there, gathered round him with admiring eyes, and escorted him down the street.

"Give us a tune, Christie; play away, Christie," they all cried out. But Christie shook his head resolutely, and marched on. He was not sorry when they grew tired of following him and turned back. Now he felt himself a man; and he went on in a most independent manner.

And then he began to play. What a moment that was for him!

He had often turned the handle of the barrel-organ in the lonely old attic, but that was a very different thing to playing it in the street. There had been no one to hear him there but old Treffy, who used to stand by anxiously, saying, "Turn her gently, Christie; turn her gently." But here there were crowds of people passing by, and sometimes someone stopped for a minute, and then how proud Christie felt! There was no barrel-organ like this, he felt sure. He did not care what the folks said about "Marshall Lazy"; he was not so good as *Poor Mary Ann*, Christie felt sure; and as for *Home, sweet Home*, Christie almost broke down every time he played it. He did *so* love his mother,

16

and he could not help thinking she was singing it still somewhere. He wondered very much where she was, and where "Home sweet Home" was. He must try and find out somehow.

And thus the day wore away, and Christie's patience was rewarded by quite a little store of pence. How proud he was to spend it on his way home in comforts for old Treffy, and how much he enjoyed giving the old man an account of his day's adventures.

Treffy gave Christie a warm welcome when he opened the attic door; but it would be hard to say whether he was more pleased to see Christie, or to see his dear old barrel-organ. He examined it most carefully and tenderly, but he could not discover that Christie had done any harm to it, and he praised him accordingly.

Then, whilst Christie was getting tea ready, Treffy played through all his four tunes, dwelling most affectionately and admiringly on *Home, sweet Home.*

3
Only Another Month

OLD TREFFY did not regain his strength. He continued weak and feeble. He was not actually ill, and could sit up day after day by the tiny fire which Christie lit for him in the morning. But he was not able to descend the steep staircase, much less to walk about with the heavy organ, which even made Christie's shoulders ache.

So Christie took the old man's place. It was not always such pleasant work as on that first morning. There were cold days and rainy days; there was drizzling sleet, which lashed Christie's face; and biting frost which chilled him through and through. There were damp fogs, which wrapped him round like a wet blanket, and rough winds, which nearly took him off his feet.

Then he grew a little weary of the sound of the poor old organ. He never had the heart to confess this to old Treffy; indeed he scarcely liked to own it to himself; but he could not help wishing that *Poor Mary Ann* would come to the end of her troubles, and that the *Old Hundredth* would change into something new. He never grew tired of *Home, sweet Home*, it was ever fresh to him, for he heard in it his mother's voice.

Thus the winter wore away, and the spring came on and the days became longer and lighter. Then Christie would go much farther out of the town, to the quiet suburbs where the sound of a barrel-organ was not so often heard. The people had time to listen in these parts; they were far away from the busy stir of the town, and there were but few passers-by on the pavement. It was rather dull in these outlying suburbs. The rows of villas, with their stiff gardens in front, grew a little monotonous. It was just the kind of place in which a busy, active mind would long

18

for a little variety. And so it came to pass that even a barrel-organ was a welcome visitor; and one and another would throw Christie a penny, and encourage him to come again.

One hot spring day, when the sun was shining in all his vigour, as if he had been tired of being hidden in the winter, Christie was toiling up one of the roads on the outskirts of the town. The organ was very heavy for him, and he had to stop every now and then to rest for a minute. At length he reached a nice-looking house, standing in a very pretty garden. The flower-beds in front of the house were filled with the early spring flowers; snowdrops, crocuses, violets, and hepaticas were in full bloom.

Before this house Christie began to play. He could have hardly have told why he chose it; perhaps he had no reason for doing so, except that it had such a pretty garden in front, and Christie always loved flowers. His mother had once bought him a penny bunch of spring flowers, which, after living for many days in a broken bottle, Christie had pressed in an old spelling-book, and, through all his troubles, he had never parted with them.

And thus, before the house with the pretty garden, Christie began to play. He had not turned the handle of the organ three times, before two merry little faces appeared at a window at the top of the house, and watched him with lively interest. They put their heads out of the window as far as the protecting bars would allow them, and Christie could hear all they said.

"Look at him," said the little girl, who seemed to be about five years old; "doesn't he turn it nicely, Charlie?"

"Yes, he does," said Charlie, "and what a pretty tune he's playing!"

"Yes," said the little girl, "it's so cheerful, Isn't it, Nurse," she added, turning round to the girl who was holding her by the waist to prevent her falling out of the window. Mabel had heard her papa make a similar remark to her mamma the night before when she had been playing a piece of music to him for the first time, and she therefore thought it was the correct way to express her admiration of Christie's tune.

But the tune happened to be *Poor Mary Ann*, the words of which Nurse knew very well indeed. And as Mary Ann was Nurse's own name, she had grown quite sentimental whilst Charlie was playing it, and had been wondering whether John Brown, the grocer's young man, who had promised to be faithful to her for ever and ever more, would ever behave to her as poor Mary Ann's lover did, and leave her to die forlorn. Thus she could not quite agree with Miss Mabel's remark, that *Poor Mary Ann* was so cheerful, and she seemed rather relieved when the tune changed to *Rule Britannia*. But when *Rule Britannia* was finished, and the organ began *Home sweet Home*, the children fairly screamed with delight; for their mother had often sung it to them, and they recognized it as an old favourite; and with their pretty, childish voices, they joined in the chorus: "Home, sweet Home, there's no place like home, there's no place like home." And as poor Christie looked up at them, it seemed to him that they, at least, *did* know something of what they sang.

"Why have I not a nice home?" he wondered. But the children had run away from the window, and scampered downstairs to ask their mamma for some money for the poor organ-boy. A minute afterwards two pennies were thrown to Christie from the nursery window. They fell down into the middle of a bed of pure white snowdrops, and Christie had to open the garden gate, and walk cautiously over the grass to pick them up. But for some time he could not find them, for they were hidden by the flowers; so the children ran downstairs again to help him. At last the pennies were discovered, and Christie took off his hat and made a low bow, as they presented them to him. He put the money in his pocket and looked lovingly down on the snowdrops.

"They *are* pretty flowers, missie," he said.

"Would you like one, organ-boy?" asked Mabel, standing

on tip-toe, and looking into Christie's face.

"Could you spare one?" said Christie, eagerly.

"I'll ask Mamma," said Mabel, and she ran into the house.

"I'm to gather four," she said, when she came back: "organ-boy, you shall choose."

It was a weighty matter selecting the flowers; and then the four snowdrops were tied together and given to Christie.

"My mother once gave me some like these, missie," he said.

"Does she never give you any now?" said Mabel.

"No, missie, she's dead," said Christie, mournfully.

"Oh!" said little Mabel in a sorrowful, pitying voice, "poor organ-boy, poor organ-boy!"

Christie now put his organ on his back and prepared to depart.

"Ask him what his name is," whispered Mabel to Charlie.

"No, no; you ask him."

"*Please*, Charlie, ask him," said Mabel again.

"What is your name, organ-boy?" said Charlie, shyly.

Christie told them his name, and as he went down the road he heard their voices calling after him -

"Come again, Christie; come again another day, Christie; come again soon, Christie."

The snowdrops were very faded and withered when Christie reached the attic that night. He tried to revive them in water, but they would not look fresh again; so he laid them to rest beside his mother's faded flowers in the old spelling-book.

Christie was not long in repeating his visit to the suburban road, but this time, though he played his four tunes twice through, and lingered regretfully over *Home sweet Home*, he saw nothing of the children, and received neither smiles nor snowdrops. For Mabel and Charlie had gone for a long country walk with their nurse, and were far away from the sound of poor Christie's organ.

Treffy was still unable to get out, and he grew rather fretful sometimes, even with Christie. It was very dull for him sitting alone all day; and he had nothing to comfort him, not even his old friend the organ. And when Christie came home at night, if the store of pence was not so large as usual, poor old Treffy would sigh, and moan, and wish he could get about again, and take his old organ out as before.

But Christie bore it very patiently, for he loved his old master more than he had loved anyone since his mother died; and love can bear many things. Still, he did wish he could find someone or something to comfort Treffy, and to make him better.

"Master Treffy," he said, one night, "shall I fetch the doctor to you?"

"No, no, Christie, boy," said Treffy; "let me be, let me be."

But Christie was not to be so easily put off. What if Treffy should die, and leave him alone in the world again? The little attic, dismal though it was, had been a home to Christie, and it had been good to have some one to love him once again. He would be very, very lonely if Treffy died; and the old man was growing very thin and pale, and his hands were very trembling and feeble; he could scarcely turn the old organ now. And Christie had heard of old people "breaking up", as it is called, and then going off suddenly; and he began to be very much afraid old Treffy would do the same. He *must* get someone to come and see his old master.

The landlady of the house had fallen downstairs and broken her arm; a doctor came to see *her*, Christie knew; oh, if he would only step upstairs and look at old Treffy! It was such a little way from the landlady's room to the attic, and it would only take him a few minutes. And then Christie could ask him what was the matter with the old man, and whether old Treffy would get better.

These thoughts kept Christie awake a long time that night; he turned restlessly on his pillow, and felt very troubled and anxious. The moonlight streamed into the room, and fell on old Treffy's face as he lay on his bed in the corner. Christie raised himself on his elbow, and looked at him. Yes, he *did* look very wasted and ill. Oh, how he hoped Treffy would not go away, as his mother had done, and leave him behind!

The next day he watched about on the stairs till the land-lady's doctor came. Old Treffy thought him very idle because he would not go out with the organ; but Christie put him off with first one excuse and then another, and kept looking out of the window and down the court, that he might see the doctor's carriage stop at the entrance.

When at last the doctor came, Christie watched him go into the landlady's room and sat at the door till he came out. He shut the door quickly after him, and was running down the steps, when he heard an eager voice calling after him.

"Please, sir, please, sir," said Christie.

"Well, my boy, what do you want?" said the doctor.

"Please, sir - don't be cross, sir, but if you *would* walk upstairs a minute into the attic, sir; it's old Treffy, and he's ever so poorly."

"Who *is* old Treffy?" asked the doctor.

"He's my old master; that's to say, he takes care of me - at least it's me that takes care of him, please, sir."

The doctor did not quite know what to make of this lucid explanation. However, he turned round and began slowly to ascend the attic stairs.

"What's the matter with him?" he asked, kindly.

"That's what I want to know, sir," said Christie; "he's a very old man, sir, and I'm afraid he won't live long, and I want to know, please. But I'd better go in first, please, sir; Master Treffy doesn't know you're coming. Master Treffy," said Christie, walking bravely into the room, "here's the landlady's doctor come to see you."

And to Christie's great joy, old Treffy made no objection, but submitted very patiently and gently to the doctor's investigations, without even asking who had sent him. And, the doctor took leave, promising to send some medicine in the morning, and walked out into the close court. He was just getting into his carriage, when he felt a little cold hand on his arm.

"Please, sir, how much is it?" said Christie's voice.

"How much is what?" asked the doctor.

"How much is it for coming to see poor old Treffy, sir? I've got a few coppers here, sir," said Christie, bringing them out of his pocket; "will these be enough, sir? or, if not, sir, I'll bring some more to your house to-morrow."

"Oh," said the doctor, smiling, "you may keep your money, boy; I won't take your last penny, and when I come to see Mrs. White I'll give a look at the old man again."

Christie looked, but did not speak his thanks.

"Please, sir, what do you think of Master Treffy?" he asked.

"He won't be here long, boy - perhaps another month or so," said the doctor, as he drove away.

"A month or so! Only a month!" said Christie to himself, as he walked slowly back, with a dead weight on his soul. A month more with his dear old master - only another month, only another month. And in the minute which passed before Christie reached the attic, he saw, as in a sorrowful picture, what life would be to him without old Treffy. He would have no home, not even the old attic; he would have no friend. *No home, no friend; no friend!* That would be his sorrow. And only another month before it came! Only another month!

It was with a dull, heavy heart that Christie opened the attic door.

"Christie, boy," said old Treffy's voice, "what did the doctor say?"

"He said you had only another month, Master Treffy," sobbed Christie, "only another month; and whatever shall I do without you?"

Treffy did not speak; it was a solemn thing to be told he had only another month to live; that in another month he must leave Christie and the attic and the old organ, and go - he knew not whither. It was a solemn, searching thought for old Treffy.

He spoke very little all day. Christie stayed at home, for he had not heart enough to take the organ out that sorrowful day; and he watched old Treffy very gently and mournfully. *Only another month! Only another month!* was ringing in the ears of both.

But when the evening came on, and there was no light in the room but what came from the handful of fire in the grate, old Treffy began to talk.

"Christie," he said, uneasily, "where am I going? Where shall I be in a month, Christie?"

Christie gazed into the fire thoughtfully.

"My mother talked about heaven, Master Treffy; and she said she was going home. *Home sweet Home*, that was the last thing she sang. I expect that 'Home sweet Home' is somewhere in heaven, Master Treffy; I expect so. It's a good place, so my mother said."

"Yes," said old Treffy, "I suppose it is; but I can't help thinking I shall be very strange there, Christie, very strange indeed. I know so little about it, so very little, Christie, boy."

"Yes," said Christie, "and I don't know much."

"And I don't know any one there, Christie; you won't be there, nor any one that I know; and I shall have to leave my poor old organ; you don't suppose they'll have any barrel organs there will they, Christie?"

"No," said Christie, "I never heard my mother speak of any; I think she said they played on harps in heaven."

"I shan't like that *half* so well," said old Treffy, sorrowfully; "I don't know how I shall pass my time."

Christie did not know what to say to this, so he made no answer.

"Christie, boy," said old Treffy, suddenly "I want you to make out about heaven, I want you to find out all about it for me; maybe, I shouldn't feel so strange there, if I knew what I was going to; and your mother called it 'Home, sweet Home', didn't she?"

"Yes," said Christie, "I'm sure it was heaven she meant."

"Now, Christie, boy, mind you make out," said Treffy, earnestly; "and remember there's only another month! Only another month!"

"I'll do my best, Master Treffy," said Christie, "I'll do my very best."

And Christie kept his word.

4
Mabel's First Lesson in Organ Grinding

THE next day Christie had to go out as usual. Old Treffy seemed no worse than before - he was able to sit up, and Christie opened the small window before he went out to let a breath of fresh air into the close attic. But there was very little fresh air anywhere that day. The atmosphere was heavy and stifling, and poor Christie's heart felt depressed and weary. He turned, he hardly knew why, to the surburban road, and stopped before the house with the pretty garden. He wanted to see those merry little faces again - perhaps they would cheer him; he felt so very dull to-day.

Christie was not disappointed this time. He had hardly turned the handle of the organ twice before Mabel and Charlie appeared at the nursery window; and after satisfying themselves that it really *was* Christie, their own organ-boy, they ran into the garden, and stood beside him as he played.

"Doesn't he turn it nicely?" whispered Charlie to his sister.

"Yes," said little Mabel; "I wish I had an organ, don't you, Charlie?"

"Shall I ask Papa to buy us one?" asked her brother.

"I don't know, Charlie, if Mamma would like it always," said Mabel. "She has such bad headaches, you know."

"Well; but up in the nursery she would hardly hear it, I'm sure," said Charlie, regretfully.

"I *should* so like to turn it," said Mabel, shyly, looking up into Christie's face.

"All right, missie; come here," said Christie.

And standing on tip-toe at his side, little Mabel took hold of the handle of the organ with her tiny white hand. Very slowly and carefully she turned it, so slowly that her mamma came to the window to see if the organ-boy had suddenly been taken ill.

It was a pretty sight which that young mother looked upon. The little fair, delicate child, in her light summer dress, turning the handle of the old, faded barrel-organ, and the organ-boy standing by, watching her with admiring eyes. Then little Mabel looked up, and saw her mother's face at the window, and smiled and nodded to her, delighted to find that she was watching. And then Mabel went on playing with a happy consciousness that Mother was listening. For there was no one in the world that little Mabel loved so much as her mother.

But Mabel turned so slowly that she grew tired of the melancholy wails of *Poor Mary Anne*.

"Change it, please, organ-boy," she said; "make it play *Home, sweet Home* - Mother *does* like that so."

But Christie knew that *Rule Britannia* lay between that and *Home, sweet Home*; so he took the handle from Mabel, and saying, brightly, "All right, missie, I'll make it come as quick as I can," he turned it round so fast, that if old Treffy had been within hearing, he would certainly have died from fright about his dear old organ, long before the month was over. Several people in the opposite houses came to their windows to look out; they thought the organ must be possessed with some evil spirit, so slowly did it go one minute, so quickly the next.

But they understood how it was a minute afterwards when little Mabel again began to turn, and very slowly and deliberately the first notes of *Home, sweet Home* were sounded forth. She turned the handle of the organ until *Home, sweet Home* was quite finished, and then, with a sigh of satisfaction, she gave it up to Christie.

"I like *Home, sweet Home*," she said; "it's such a pretty tune."

"Yes," said Christie, "it's my favourite, missie.

28

Where is 'Home, sweet Home,'?" he asked suddenly as he remembered his promise to old Treffy.

"That's *my* home," said little Mabel, nodding her head in the direction of the pretty house. "I don't know where yours is, Christie."

"I haven't much of a place to call home, missie," said Christie; "me and old Treffy we live together in an old attic, and that won't be for long - only another month, Miss Mabel, and I shall have no home then."

"Poor organ-boy - poor Christie!" said little Mabel, in a pitying voice.

Charlie had taken the handle of the organ now, and was rejoicing in *Poor Mary Ann*; but Mabel hardly listened to him; she was thinking of the poor boy who had no home but an attic, and who soon would have no home at all.

"There's another home somewhere," said Christie, "isn't there, missie? Isn't heaven some sort of a home?"

"Oh yes, there's heaven," said little Mabel brightly; "you'll have a home *there*, won't you, organ-boy?"

"Where is heaven?" said Christie.

"It's up there," said little Mabel, pointing up to the sky; "up so high, Christie. The little stars live in heaven; I used to think they were the angels' eyes, but Nurse says it's silly to think that."

"I like the stars," said Christie.

"Yes," said Mabel, "so do I; and you'll see them all when you go to heaven, Christie, I'm sure you will."

"What is heaven like, Miss Mabel? asked Christie.

"Oh, it's so nice," said little Mabel; "they have white dresses on, and the streets are all gold, Christie, all gold and shining. And Jesus is there, Christie - wouldn't you like to see Jesus?" she added in a whisper.

"I don't know," said Christie, in a bewildered tone; "I don't know much about Him."

"Don't you love Jesus, Christie?" said Mabel, with a very

grave, sorrowful face, and with tears in her large, brown eyes. "Oh, organ-boy, don't you love Jesus?"

"No," said Christie; "I know so little about Him, Miss."

"But you can't go to heaven if you don't love Jesus, Christie. Oh, I'm so sorry - you won't have a home at all; what *will* you do?" and the tears ran down little Mabel's cheeks.

But just then the bell rang for dinner, and Nurse's voice called the children in.

Christie walked on very thoughtfully. He was thinking of little Mabel's words and little Mabel's tears. "You can't go to heaven if you don't love Jesus," she had said; "and then you won't have a home at all." It was a new thought for Christie, and a very sad thought. What if he should never, never know anything of "Home, sweet Home"? And then came the remembrance of poor old Treffy, his dear old master, who had only another month to live. Did he love Jesus? He had never heard old Treffy mention His name; and what if Treffy should die, and never go to heaven at all, but go to the other place! Christie had heard of hell; he did not know much about it, and he had always fancied it was for very bad people. He must tell Treffy about Mabel's words. Perhaps, after all, his old master did love Jesus. Christie hoped very much that he did. He longed for evening to come, that he might go home and ask him.

The afternoon was still more close and sultry than the morning had been, and little Christie was weary. The organ was heavy for him at all times, and it seemed heavier than usual to-day. He was obliged to sit down to rest for a few minutes on a door-step in one of the back streets, about half a mile from the court where old Treffy lived. As he was sitting there, with his organ resting against the wall, two women met each other just in front of the door-step, and after asking most affectionately after each other's health, they began to talk, and Christie could not help hearing every word they said.

"What's that place?" said one of them, looking across the road at a long, low building with a board in front of it.

"Oh, that's our new mission-room, Mrs. West," said the other; "it belongs to the church at the corner of Melville Street. A young man comes and preaches there every Sunday night; I like to hear him, I do," she went on, "he puts it so plain."

"Puts what plain, Mrs. Smith?" said her friend.

"Oh, all about heaven, and how we're to get there, and about Jesus, and what He's done for us. He's a kind man, is Mr. Wilton; he came to see our Tommy when he was badly. Do you know him, Mrs. West?"

"No," said Mrs. West; "maybe I'll come to-morrow; what time is it?"

"It begins at seven o'clock every Sunday," said Mrs. Smith; "and you needn't bother about your clothes - there's no one there but poor folks like ourselves."

"Well, I'll come, Mrs. Smith. Good day;" and the two parted.

And little Christie had heard all they said, and had firmly made up his mind to be at the mission-room the next evening at seven o'clock. He must lose no time in making out what Treffy wanted to know. One day of the month was gone already.

"Master Treffy," said Christie that night, "do you love Jesus?"

"Jesus!" said the old man; "no, Christie, I can't say I do. I suppose I ought to: good folk do, don't they?"

"Master Treffy," said Christie solemnly, "if you don't love Jesus you can't go to heaven, and you'll never have a home any more - never any more."

"Ay, ay, Christie, that's true, I'm afraid. When I was a little chap no bigger than you, I used to hear tell about these things. But I gave no heed to them then, and I've forgotten all I ever heard. I've been thinking a deal lately since I was took so bad; and some of it seems to come back to me. But I can't rightly mind what I was told. It's a bad job, Christie, a bad job."

5
No Sin in the City Bright

IT had been a close, sultry day, and it was a still more oppressive night. It was long before Christie could get to sleep, and when at last he had sunk into a troubled slumber, he was woken suddenly by a loud peal of thunder, which made the old attic shake from end to end.

Old Treffy raised himself in bed, and Christie crept to his side. It was an awful storm; the lightning flashed into the attic, lighting up for a moment every corner of it, and showing Christie old Treffy's white and trembling face. Then all was dark again, and there came the heavy roll of the thunder, which sounded like the noise of falling houses, and which made old Treffy shake from head to foot. Christie never remembered such a storm before, and he was very much afraid. He knelt very close to his old master, and took hold of his trembling hand.

"Are you frightened, Master Treffy?" he asked at last, as a vivid flash again darted into the room.

"Yes, Christie, boy," said old Treffy; "I don't know how it is; I used not to be afraid of a storm, but I am to-night."

Poor Christie did not speak, so Treffy went on -

"The lightning seems like God looking at me, Christie, and the thunder seems like God's voice, and I am afraid of Him. I don't love Him, Christie, I don't love Him."

And again the lightning flashed and the thunder rolled, and again old Treffy shook from head to foot.

"I shouldn't like to die to-night, Christie," he said; "and the lightning comes so very near me. Christie, boy, do you know what sin is?" he whispered.

"Yes," said Christie; "it's doing wrong things, isn't it?"

"Yes," said Treffy, "and I've done a many of them, Christie; and it's thinking bad thoughts, and I've thought a many of them, Christie; and it's saying bad words, and I've said a many of them, Christie. But I never cared about it before to-night."

"How did you come to care about it to-night?" asked Christie.

"I've had a dream, Christie, boy, and it has made me tremble.

"Tell me it, Master Treffy," pleaded Christie.

"I was thinking of what you said about loving Jesus, and I fell asleep, and I thought I was standing before a beautiful gate; it was made of gold, Christie, and over the gate there were some shining letters. I spelt them out, and they were 'Home, sweet Home', Christie, and I said to myself, 'I've found it at last: I wish Christie was here.' But just then someone opened the gate and said, 'What do you want, old man?' 'I want to come in,' I said, 'I'm very tired, and I want to be at home.' But he shut the gate, and said to me very gravely and sorrowfully, 'No sin can come in here, old Treffy; no sin can come in here.' And, Christie, I felt as if I was nothing but sin, so I turned round and walked away, and it grew very dark. And just then came the thunder, and I awoke with a start. I can't forget it, Christie; I can't forget it," said old Treffy.

And still the lightning flashed and the thunder rolled, and still old Treffy trembled.

Christie could not comfort him, for he was very much afraid himself, but he pressed very close up to his side, and did not leave him till the storm was over, and there was no sound but the heavy downpour of the rain on the roof of the attic. Then he crept back to bed and fell asleep.

The next morning it all seemed like a bad dream. The sun was shining brightly, and Christie rose and opened the attic window. Everything looked fresh and clean after the rain. The dull, heavy feeling was gone out of the air, and the little sparrows were chirping in the eaves. It was Sunday morning, and on Sunday evening Christie was to hear the clergyman preach in the mission-room. Oh, how he wished it was seven o'clock, that he might go and find out what old Treffy wanted to know!

The poor old man seemed very restless and unhappy all that long spring day. Christie never left him, for it was only on Sunday that he could watch beside his dear old master. He could see that old Treffy had not forgotten his dream, though he did not speak of it again.

And at last the long, weary day wore away, and at six o'clock Christie washed himself and prepared to depart.

"Be sure you mind every word he says, Christie, boy," said old Treffy, earnestly.

The mission-room was only just open when little Christie arrived. A woman was inside lighting the gas and preparing the place for the congregation. Christie peeped shyly in at the door, and she caught sight of him and ordered him off.

"Isn't there going to be any preaching to-night?" said Christie, in a disappointed voice.

"Oh, you've come to the service, have you?" said the woman. "All right, you can come in, only you must sit still, and you mustn't talk or make a noise."

Now, as poor Christie had no one to talk to, this was rather an unnecessary speech. However, he went in very meekly, and sat down on one of the front benches.

Then the congregation began to arrive: old men and little children; mothers with babies in their arms; old women with shawls over their heads; husbands and wives; a few young men; people with all kinds of faces, and all kinds of characters, from the quiet and respectable artisan's wife to the poor little beggar girl who sat on the form beside Christie.

And as seven o'clock struck, the door opened and the minister came in. Christie never took his eyes off him during the whole service. And, oh, how he enjoyed the singing, the last hymn especially! A young woman behind him was singing it

34

very distinctly, and he could hear every word. Oh, if he could only have remembered it to repeat to old Treffy! The words of the hymn were as follows -

There is a city bright,
Closed are its gates to sin,
Nought that defileth,
Nought that defileth,
Can ever enter in.

Saviour, I come to Thee,
O Lamb of God, I pray,
Cleanse me and save me,
Cleanse me and save me,
Wash all my sins away.

Lord, make me from this hour
Thy loving child to be,
Kept by Thy power,
Kept by Thy power,
From all that grieveth Thee.

Till in the snowy dress
Of Thy redeemed I stand,
Faultless and stainless,
Faultless and stainless,
Safe in that happy land!

And after the hymn came the sermon. The clergyman's text was Revelation 21 : 27, "There shall in no wise enter into it anything that defileth."

He spoke of the Heavenly City of which they had just been singing, the bright, beautiful city, with its streets of gold and gates of pearl. He spoke of the river of the water of life, and the trees on either side of the river. He spoke of those who live in that happy place, of their white robes and crowns of gold, of the sweet songs they ever sing, and the joy in all their faces.

The clergyman also told them that in that bright city sorrow was never found. No weeping there, no tears, no sighs, no trouble. No tired feet on that golden pavement, no hungry ones there, no hot burning sun, no cold, frost or snow. No sickness there, and no death, no funerals in heaven, no graves in the golden city. Perfect love there, no more quarrelling or strife, no angry tones or discordant murmurs, no rude, rough voices to disturb the peace. And all this for ever and ever, no dread of its coming to an end, no gloomy fears for the future, no partings there, no good-byes. Once there, safe for ever. At home, at rest, with God.

"Would you like to go there?" asked the clergyman'.

And a quiet murmur passed through the room, a sigh of longing, an expression of assent. And little Christie whispered softly to himself, "Like to go there! Ay, that I would, me and old Treffy and all."

"'There shall in no wise enter into it anything that defileth,'" said the clergyman's voice. "'Closed are its gates to sin.' My friends, if there is *one* sin on your soul, heaven's gates will be closed against you. 'Nought that defileth, nought that defileth can ever enter in.' If all my life I had never sinned - if all my life I had never done a wicked deed, or spoken a wicked word, or thought a wicked thought; if all my life I had done everything I ought to have done, and had been perfectly sinless and holy, and yet to-night I was to commit *one* sin, that sin, however small a sin in man's eyes - *that* sin would be quite enough to shut me out of heaven. The gates would be shut against me for that one sin. No soul on which there is a speck of sin can go into that bright city."

"Is there one in this room," asked the clergyman, "who can say that he has only sinned once? Is there one here who can say that there is only *one* sin on his soul?"

And again there was a faint murmur round the room, and again a deep-drawn sigh; but this time it was the suppressed sigh of accusing consciences.

"No," said the clergyman, "there is not one of us who can say that. Every one of us has sinned again and again and again.

And each sin is like a dark blot, a deep ink stain on the soul."

"Oh!" said little Christie, in his heart, as he listened to these words; "whatever will me and Master Treffy do?"

And Christie's thoughts wandered to the lonely attic, and to old Treffy's sad, worn-out face. "So it was all true," he said to himself. "Miss Mabel's words, and Master Treffy's dream; all too true, all too true."

If Christie had been listening he would have heard the clergyman tell of the way in which sin could be taken away; but his little mind was full of the one idea of the sermon, and when he next heard the clergyman's words he was telling his congregation that he hoped they would all be present on the following Sunday evening, as he intended then to preach on the second verse of the hymn, and to tell them, more fully than he had time to do to-night, what was the only way to enter within the gates into the city.

Christie walked home very sadly and sorrowfully; he was in no haste to meet old Treffy's anxious, inquiring eyes. And when he reached the dark attic he sat down by Treffy, and looked away from him into the fire, as he said, mournfully -

"Your dream was quite right, Master Treffy. I've heard it all over again to-night. He preached about it, and we sang about it, so there's no mistake now."

"Tell me all, Christie, boy," said Treffy, pitifully.

"It's a beautiful place, Master Treffy," said Christie; "you'd be ever so happy and comfortable if you could only get there. But there's no sin allowed inside the gates; that's what the clergyman said, and what the hymn said, too -

> There is a city bright,
> Closed are its gates to sin."

"Then there's no chance for me, Christie," said the old man, "no chance for me."

And hours after that, when Christie thought Treffy was fast asleep on his bed in the corner, he heard his poor old trembling voice murmuring again and again:

"'Closed are its gates to sin, closed are its gates to sin.'"

And there was another ear listening to old Treffy's voice. The man at the gate, of whom Bunyan writes, had heard the old man's sorrowful wail, and it went to his very heart. He knew all about old Treffy, and he was soon to say to him, with tones of love, as he opened the gate of rest: "I am willing with all my heart to let thee in."

6
The Only Way into "Home, Sweet Home"

THAT week was a very long and sorrowful one to Treffy and to Christie. The old man seldom spoke, except to murmur the sad words of the hymn, or to say to Christie, in a despairing voice -

"It's all up with me, Christie, boy; no home for me."

The barrel-organ was quite neglected by Treffy, Christie took it out in the day-time, but at night it stood against the wall untouched. Treffy could not bear to hear it now. Christie had begun to turn it one evening, but the first tune it had played was *Home, sweet Home*, and Treffy had said bitterly -

"Don't play that, Christie, boy; there's no 'Home, sweet Home' for me; I shall never have a home again, never again."

So Treffy had nothing to comfort him. Even his old organ seemed to have taken part against him; even his dear old organ, which he had loved so much, had helped to make him more miserable.

The doctor had looked into the attic again, according to his promise, but he said there was nothing to be done for Treffy, it was only a question of time, no medicine could save his life.

It was a very terrible thing for old Treffy thus to be slipping away, each day the chain of his life becoming looser and looser, and he drawing near each day to - he knew not what.

Treffy and Christie were counting anxiously the days to Sunday, when they would hear about the second verse of the hymn. Perhaps after all there might be some hope, some way into the bright city, some entrance into "Home, sweet Home",

39

through which even old Treffy's sin-stained soul might pass.

And at last Sunday came. It was a wet, rainy night, the wind was high and stormy, and the little congregation in the mission room was smaller than usual. But there was an earnest purpose in the faces of many who came, and the clergyman, as he looked round at the little company when he gave out his text, felt that many of them had not come from mere curiosity, but from an honest desire to hear the Word of God. And he lifted up his heart in very earnest prayer, that to many in that room the Word which he was about to speak might be a lasting blessing.

The mission-room was very still when the minister gave out his text. Little Christie's eyes were fixed intently on him, and he listened eagerly for every word.

The text was this: "The blood of Jesus Christ, His Son, cleanseth us from all sin."

The clergyman first reminded them of his last Sunday's sermon, of the bright golden city where they all longed to be. He reminded them of the first verse of the hymn -

> There is a city bright,
> Closed are its gates to sin.

And then he asked very gently and tenderly, "Is there anyone in this room who has come here to-night longing to know of some way in which he, a sinner, can enter the city? Is there such a one here?"

"Ay," said little Christie under his breath, "there's me."

"I will try, by God's help, to show you the way," said the clergyman. "You and I have sinned. One sin is enough to shut us out of heaven, but we have sinned, not once only, but hundreds of thousands of times; our souls are covered with sin-stains. But there is one thing, and only one, by which the soul can be made white and clear and pure. My text tells us what it is - 'The blood of Jesus Christ.'"

Then the clergyman went on to explain how it is that the blood of Jesus can wash out sin. He spoke of the death of Jesus on Calvary, of the fountain He opened there for sin and for uncleanness. He explained to them that Jesus was God's Son, and that therefore His blood which He shed on the cross is of infinite value. He told them that, since that day on Calvary, thousands had come to the fountain, and each one had come out of it whiter than snow, every spot of sin gone.

The clergyman told them that when these washed ones reached the gates of pearl, they were thrown wide open to them, for there was no sin-mark on their souls, they were free from sin. And then he looked very earnestly indeed, and leaning forward he pleaded with his little congregation to come to the blood that they might be washed and cleansed. He begged them to use the second verse of the hymn, and say from the bottom of their hearts -

> Saviour, I come to Thee,
> O Lamb of God, I pray,
> Cleanse me and save me,
> Cleanse me and save me,
> Wash all my sins away.

"There is one little word in my text," said the minister, "which is a great comfort to me - I mean the word *all.* All sin. That takes in every bad word, every bad thought, every bad action. That takes in the blackest blot, the darkest stain, the deepest spot. All sin, each sin, every sin. No sin too bad for the blood to reach. No sin too great for the blood to cover. And now," said the minister, "every soul in this room is either saved or unsaved, either washed or not washed.

"Let me ask you, my dear friends, a very solemn question: Is the sin or the blood on your soul? One or the other must be there. Which is it?"

The clergyman paused a moment when he had asked this question, and the room was so still that a falling pin might have been heard. There were deep searchings of heart in that little company. And Christie was saying deep down in his heart -

> Cleanse me and save me,
> Cleanse me and save me,
> Wash all my sins away.

41

The minister finished his sermon by entreating them all that very night to come to the fountain. Oh, how earnestly he pleaded with them to delay no longer, but to say at once, "Saviour, I come to Thee." He begged them to go home, and in their own rooms to kneel down feeling that Jesus was standing close beside them. "That is *coming* to Jesus," the minister said. He told them to tell Jesus all, to turn all the sin over to Him, to ask Him to cover it all with His blood, so that that very night they might lie down to sleep whiter than snow.

"Will you do this?" asked the clergyman, anxiously; "will you?"

And little Christie said in his heart, "Yes, that I will."

As the congregation left, the clergyman stood at the door giving a friendly word to each one as they passed by. He looked very tired and anxious after his sermon. It had been preached with much prayer and with much feeling, and he was longing, oh, so earnestly, to know that it had been blessed to one soul.

There were some amongst the little congregation who passed by him with serious, thoughtful faces, and as each one went by he breathed an earnest prayer that the seed in that soul might spring up and bring forth fruit. But there were others again who had already begun to talk to their neighbours, and who seemed to have forgotten all they had heard. And these filled the young minister's heart with sorrow. "Is the seed lost, dear Lord?" he said, faithlessly, for he was very tired and weary, and when the body is weak our faith is apt to grow weak also.

But there was something in Christie's face as he passed out of the room which made the clergyman call him back and speak to him. He had noticed the boy's attention during his sermon, and he had longed to hear whether he had understood what he had heard.

"My boy," said the minister, kindly, laying his hand on Christie's shoulder, "can you tell me what my text was to-night?"

Christie repeated it very correctly, and the clergyman seemed pleased. He asked Christie several more questions about the sermon, and then he encouraged the boy to talk to him. Christie told him of old Treffy, who had only another month to live, and who was longing to know how he might go to "Home, sweet Home". The clergyman promised to come and see him, and wrote down the name of the court and the number of the house in his little brown pocket-book. And before Christie went home the clergyman knelt down with him in the empty mission-room, and prayed that that very night the dear Lord would wash Christie's soul in His most precious blood.

Christie walked away very thoughtfully, but still very gladly, for he had good news for old Treffy to-night. He quickened his steps as he drew near the court, and ran up the stairs to the attic eager to tell all to the poor old man.

"Oh, Master Treffy!" said Christie; "I've had such a time! It was beautiful, Master Treffy, and the clergyman's been talking to me, and he's coming to see you; he's coming here," said Christie, triumphantly.

But Treffy was longing for better news than this.

"What about 'Home, sweet Home', Christie?" he asked.

"There *is* a way, Master Treffy," said Christie. "You and me can't get in with our sins, but 'The blood of Jesus Christ, God's Son, cleanseth us from all sin.' That's in the Bible, Master Treffy, and it was the clergyman's text."

"Tell me all about it, Christie," Treffy said, in a tremulous voice.

"There's nothing but the blood of Jesus can wash away the sin, Master Treffy," said Christie, "and you and me have just got to go to Him and ask Him, and He'll do it for us to-night; the clergyman said so. I've learnt another verse of the hymn, Master Treffy," said Christie, kneeling down beside him and repeating it reverently -

Saviour, I come to Thee,
O Lamb of God, I pray,

> Cleanse me and save me,
> Cleanse me and save me,
> Wash all my sins away.

Treffy repeated the words after him in a trembling voice.

"I wish He'd wash me, Christie boy," he said, anxiously.

"So He will, Master Treffy," said Christie; "He never sends anybody away."

"Ay, but I'm an old man, Christie, and I've been a sinner all my life, and I've done some bad things, Christie. I never knew it till this last week, but I know it now. It's not likely He'll ever wash my sins; they're ever such big ones, Christie."

"Oh, but He will," said Christie eagerly; "that's just what the clergyman said; there's a word in the text for you. Master Treffy: 'The blood of Jesus Christ, His Son, cleanseth us from *all* sin.' All sin, all sin, Master Treffy; won't that do?"

"All sin," murmured old Treffy. "all sin! Yes, Christie, I think that *will* do."

There was a pause after this. Christie sat still, looking into the fire. Then he said suddenly -

"Master Treffy, let's go right away now and ask Him."

"Ask who?" said old Treffy; "the clergyman?"

"No," said Christie, "the Lord Jesus. He's in the room - the minister said He was. Let's ask Him to wash you and me, just now, Master Treffy."

"Ay!" said old Treffy, "let's ask Him, Christie." So the old man and the boy knelt down, and with a strong realization of the Lord's near presence, little Christie prayed -

"O Lord Jesus, we come to Thee, me and Master Treffy; we've got lots of sins to be washed, but the minister said You wouldn't send us away, and the text says *all* sin. We think it means us, Lord Jesus, me and Master Treffy. Please wash us white; we want to go to 'Home, sweet Home': please wash us in the blood to-night. Amen."

Then old Treffy took up the words, and in a trembling voice, added -

"Amen, Lord; wash us both, me and Christie, wash us white. Please do. Amen."

Then they got up from their knees, and Christie said -

"We may go to bed now, Master Treffy, for I'm sure He's done it for us."

Thus the man at the gate had received both the trembling old man and the little child, and as they had entered in they had heard a gracious Voice very deep down in their hearts saying to each of them again and again, "Be of good cheer, thy sins are forgiven thee."

7
Little Mabel's Snowdrops

THE next morning Christie woke with a happy heart, for he remembered his last night's prayer, and in his simple faith he had taken the Lord at His word, and had believed that the blood of Jesus Christ had cleansed him from all sin.

But old Treffy's doubts and fears came back again. He began to look within, and the remembrance of his sin returned upon him. What if, after all, there was sin on his soul? What if the gates were still closed against him?"

"Christie, boy, I don't feel it's all right with me yet," he said anxiously.

"Why not, Master Treffy?" asked Christie.

"Why, I've been so bad, Christie; it doesn't seem likely He'd do it for me so soon as that; there's such a deal of sin on my soul."

"But you asked Him to wash you, Master Treffy: didn't you?"

"Ay, I asked Him, Christie," said Treffy, in a despairing tone.

"And He said He would if you asked Him, Master Treffy: didn't He?"

"Ay, Christie, I believe He did," said Treffy.

"Then of course He *has* done it," said Christie.

"I don't know, Christie, boy; I can't feel it," said old Treffy, pitifully. "I don't seem to see it as I ought."

So whilst little Christie was walking in the sunshine, old Treffy was still groping on in the shadow, sometimes hoping, sometimes fearing, but never trusting.

Christie paid another visit to the suburban road that week.

Little Mabel and her mother were coming out of the house when Christie reached the gate. The little girl ran eagerly forward when she caught sight of the organ, and begged her mamma to stay whilst she turned the handle just six times.

The lady spoke very kindly to Christie; she asked him several questions, and he told her about old Treffy, how ill he was, and how he had not another month to live. The tears were in the lady's eyes, and she asked Christie where he lived, and wrote it down on a white tablet which she carried in her pocket.

"Mamma," said little Mabel, "I want to whisper something to you."

The lady bent down her head to listen, and then said kindly, "Yes, if you like."

Mabel darted into the house, and returned with a large bunch of single white snowdrops, prettily arranged with sprigs of dark myrtle leaves. Very white, pure, and lovely they looked.

"Here, organ-boy," said Mabel, as she put them into his hands, "these are my own dear snowdrops; Aunt Helen gave me them, and you must take them to Master Treffy - he'll like them, won't he?" she said.

"Ay, that he will, missie," said Christie, warmly.

"Mabel," said her mother, "you must teach Christie the little prayer I told you always to say when you looked at the snowdrops."

"Yes," said Mabel, "I will. This is it, Christie: 'Wash me, and I shall be whiter than snow.'"

Christie looked up brightly.

"Will you say that prayer, Christie?" asked the lady, kindly.

"Yes, ma'am," said Christie, "its just like what me and Master Treffy said last night -

Cleanse me and save me,
Cleanse me and save me,
Wash all my sins away."

The lady smiled when Christie said this, and seemed very pleased.

47

"I am so glad you know of the only way to be washed white," said the lady. "These snowdrops always make me think of the souls washed white in the blood of Jesus."

Then the lady and little Mable passed on, and Christie looked down very tenderly on the flowers. How he *would* love them now! He turned his steps homeward at once, for he did not want the snowdrops to fade before they reached old Treffy. How fair, and clean, and pure they looked! So different to the smoke and dirt of the noisy court. Christie was almost afraid lest the thick air might soil them as he carried them through it. Some of the children ran after him and begged for a flower, but he guarded his treasures very carefully till he reached the attic.

And when Christie opened the door who should be there but the clergyman, sitting beside old Treffy, and talking to him very earnestly! He stopped to give Christie a kind word, and then he went on with what he was saying. He was telling Treffy about the death of Jesus, and how it is that the blood of Jesus can wash away all sin.

"I can't see that it's all right with me," said Treffy, in a trembling voice; "it seems dark and dim to me yet. I don't feel that I've got it; I can't feel happy."

"Treffy," said the clergyman, suddenly, "do you think I would tell you a lie?"

"No, sir," said old Treffy; "I'm sure you wouldn't; I could see it in your face, sir, if nowhere else. No, sir, I'd trust you anywhere."

"Now, Treffy," said the clergyman, taking a half-crown from his pocket, "I've brought this for you. You cannot work now, and you need many things you cannot get; I will give you this money to buy them with."

"Thank you, sir," said old Treffy, the tears running down his cheeks; "I can never thank you enough. We are very badly off just now, Christie and me."

"Stop, Treffy," said the clergyman, "it isn't yours yet - you must take it."

48

Treffy put out his trembling old hand and took the half-crown, with another murmur of thanks.

"Do you feel that you've got it, Treffy?" said the clergyman.

"Yes, sir, it's here," said old Treffy.

"Are you sure you've got it, Treffy?" said the clergyman again.

"Yes, sir," said Treffy, in a bewildered voice, "I know I have; I don't know what you mean, sir."

"I will tell you what I mean," said the clergyman. "The dear Lord Jesus has come into this room just as I have, Treffy. He has brought a gift for you, just as I did. His gift has cost Him far more than mine cost me; it has cost Him His life. He has come close to you, as I came, and He says to you, as I said: 'Old Treffy, can you trust Me? do you think I would tell you a lie?' And then He holds out His gift, as I did, Treffy, and He says, 'Take it; it is for you.' Now, Treffy, what have you to do with this gift? Just exactly what you did with mine. You have not to work for it, or wait for it. You have just to put your hand and take it. Do you know what the gift is?"

Treffy did not answer, so the clergyman went on -

"It is the forgiveness of your sin, Treffy; it is the clean heart, for which you are longing; it is the right to enter into 'Home, sweet Home', for which you have been praying, Treffy; will you take the gift?"

"I want to take it," said old Treffy, "but I don't know how."

"Did you stop to think *how* you were to take *my* gift, Treffy?"

"No," said the old man, "I just took it."

"Yes," said the clergyman, "exactly; and that is what you must do with the Lord's gift; you must just take it."

"Would it have pleased me, Treffy," said the clergyman, "if you had pulled your hand back and said, 'Oh no, sir! I don't deserve it; I don't believe you would ever give it to me, I can't take it yet?'"

"No," said Treffy, "I don't suppose it would."

"Yet this is just what you are doing to the Lord Jesus, Treffy. He is holding out His gift to you, and He wants you to take it at once, yet you hold back, and say, 'No, Lord, I can't believe what You say, I can't trust Thy word, I can't believe the gift is for me, I can't take it yet'."

"Treffy," said the clergyman, earnestly, "if you can trust me, oh, why can't you trust the Lord Jesus?"

The tears were running down the old man's face, and he could not speak.

"I am going to ask you another question, Treffy," said the clergyman. "Will you trust the Lord Jesus now?"

"Yes, sir," said Treffy, through the tears; "I don't think I can help trusting Him now."

"Now, Treffy, remember Jesus is in this attic, close to you, close to me, very, very near, Treffy. When we speak to Him He will hear every word we say; He will listen to every sigh; He will read every wish.

"But before you speak to Him, Treffy, listen to what He says to you," said the clergyman, taking his Bible from his pocket. "These are His own words, 'Come, now, and let us reason together, saith the Lord: though your sins be as scarlet, they shall be as white as snow; though they be red like crimson, they shall be as wool,' for 'The blood of Jesus Christ, His Son, cleanseth us from all sin.' Treffy, will you trust the Lord Jesus? do you think He would tell you a lie?"

"No," said old Treffy; "I'm sure He wouldn't."

"Very well, Treffy, then we will tell Him so."

The clergyman knelt down by Treffy's side, and Christie knelt down too, and old Treffy clasped his trembling hands whilst the clergyman prayed.

It was a very simple prayer; it was just taking the Lord at His word. Old Treffy repeated the words after the clergyman with the deepest earnestness, and when he had finished the old man still clasped his hands and said, "Lord Jesus, I do trust Thee, I do take the gift, I do believe Thy word."

Then the clergyman rose from his knees and said, "Treffy, when you had taken my gift, what did you do next?"

"I thanked you for it, sir," said Treffy.

"Yes," said the clergyman, "and would you not like to thank the Lord Jesus for His gift of forgiveness?"

"Oh," said Treffy, with tears in his eyes, "I should indeed, sir!"

So they all knelt down again, and in a few words the clergyman thanked the dear Lord for His great love and goodness to old Treffy, in giving him pardon for his sin.

And again old Treffy took up the words and added -

"Thank You, Lord Jesus, very much for the gift; it cost Thee Thy life; oh, I do thank Thee with all my heart!"

"Now, Treffy," said the clergyman, as he rose to go, "if Satan comes to you to-morrow, and says, 'Old Treffy, do you feel you've got forgiveness? Perhaps after all it's a mistake,' what shall you say to him?"

"I think I shall tell him my text," said old Treffy: "'The blood of Jesus Christ, His Son, cleanseth us from all sin.'"

"That will do, Treffy," said the clergyman; "he can't answer that. And remember, the Lord wishes you to *know* you are forgiven, not to *feel* you are forgiven. There is a difference between feeling and knowing. You *knew* you had taken my gift, and you did not know what I meant when I asked you if you *felt* I had given it to you. It is the same with the Lord's gift, Treffy. Your *feelings* have nothing to do with your safety, but your *faith* has a great deal to do with it. Have you taken the Lord at His word? Have you trusted Him? That is the question."

"Yes, sir," said Treffy, "I have."

"Then you *know* you are forgiven," said the clergyman, with a smile.

"Yes, sir," said Treffy, brightly, "I can trust Him now."

Then Christie walked up to Treffy, and put the bunch of white snowdrops in his hand.

"Miss Mabel gave me them," he said, "and she said I was to

say a little prayer whenever I looked at them: 'Wash me, and I shall be whiter than snow.'"

"Whiter than snow," repeated the clergyman; "whiter than snow, Treffy! That is a sweet word, is it not?"

"Yes," said old Treffy, earnestly, as he looked at the flowers, "whiter than snow, washed white in the blood of Jesus."

Then the clergyman took his leave, but as he was crossing the court he heard Christie running after him. He had a few of the lovely snowdrops and a sprig of dark myrtle in his hand.

"Please, sir," said Christie, "would you like a few of them?"

"Thank you, my boy," said the clergyman, "I should indeed."

He carried the snowdrops carefully home, and they taught him a lesson of faith. The seed he had sown in the mission-room had not been lost. Already two poor sin-stained souls had come to the fountain, and had been washed whiter than snow. The old man and the little boy had taken the Lord at His word, and had found the only way into the bright city, into "Home, sweet Home". God had been very good to him in letting him know this. Surely, he would trust in the future.

8
Made Meet for Home

HOW different everything seemed to Treffy after his doubts and fears had been removed. The very attic seemed full of sunshine, and old Treffy's heart was full of brightness. He was forgiven, and he knew it. And, as a forgiven child, he could look up into his Father's face with a smile.

A great load was taken off little Christie's heart, his old master was so happy and contented now; never impatient at his long absence when he was out with the organ, or fretful and anxious about their daily support.

Old Treffy had laid upon Jesus his load of sin, and it was not hard to lay upon Him also his load of care. The Lord who had borne the greater burden would surely bear the less. Treffy could not have put this feeling of trust into words, but he acted upon it. There were no murmurings from old Treffy now, no forebodings. He had always a bright smile and a cheerful word for Christie when the boy returned tired at night. And whilst Christie was out he would lie very still and peaceful, talking softly to himself or thanking the dear Lord for His great gift to him.

And old Treffy's trust was not disappointed. "None that trust in Him shall be desolate."

The clergyman's gift was not the only one they received that week. Christie had come home in the middle of the day to see how his old master was, and was just preparing to start again on his rounds, when he heard a gentle rustling of silk on the stairs, and a low knock at the door. Christie opened it quickly, and in walked little Mabel, and little Mabel's mamma. They had brought with them many little comforts for old Treffy, which Mabel had great pleasure in opening out. But they brought with them also what money cannot buy - sweet, gentle words, and bright smiles, which cheered old Treffy's heart.

The lady sat down beside Treffy, and they talked together of Jesus. The old man loved to talk of Jesus now, for he was able to say, "He loved me, and gave Himself for me."

And the lady took a little blue Testament from her pocket, and read a chapter to Treffy. She had a sweet, clear voice, and she read so distinctly that he could understand every word.

Little Mabel sat quite still whilst her mamma was reading, then she got up and ran across the attic.

"Here are my snowdrops," she said, with a cry of joy, as she caught sight of them in the window-sill. "Do you like them, Master Treffy?"

"Ay, little missie," said the old man, "I do, indeed, and me and Christie always think of the little prayer when we look at them."

"Wash me, and I shall be whiter than snow," repeated Mabel, reverently. "Has He washed you, Master Treffy?"

"Yes, missie," said Treffy, "I believe He has."

"I'm so glad," said little Mabel, "then you *will* go to 'Home, sweet Home'; won't he, mamma?"

"Yes," said her mother, "Treffy and Christie have found the only road which leads home. And, oh," she said, the colour coming into her sweet face, "what a happy day it will be when we all meet at home! Wouldn't you like to see Jesus, Treffy?" asked the lady.

"Ay," said old Treffy, "it would be a good sight to see His blessed face, I could almost sing for joy when I think of it, and I haven't very long to wait."

"No," said the lady, with a wistful expression in her eyes, "I could almost change places with you, Treffy; I could almost wish *I* were as near to 'Home, sweet Home.' But that would be selfish," she said brightly, as she rose to go.

But little Mable had discovered the old organ, and was in no haste to depart. She must turn it "just a little bit". In former days, old Treffy would have been seriously agitated and distressed at the idea of the handle of his dear old organ being turned by a little girl of six years old. Even now he felt a small amount of anxiety when she proposed it. But his fears vanished when he saw the careful, deliberate way in which Mabel went to work. The old organ was perfectly safe in her hands. And, to Mabel's joy, the first tune which came was *Home, sweet Home.* Very sweetly it sounded in old Treffy's ears, He was thinking of no earthly home, but of "the city bright", where he hoped soon to be. And the lady was thinking of it, too.

When the tune was finished they took their leave, and Christie looked out of the window, and watched them crossing the dirty court, and entering the carriage which was waiting for them in the street.

It had been a very bright week for Christie and for old Treffy.

And then Sunday came, and another service in the little mission-room. Christie was there in good time, and the clergyman gave him a pleasant smile as he came into the room.

It was the third verse of the hymn on which the clergyman was to preach to-night. They sang the whole hymn through before the sermon, and then they sang the third verse again, that all of them might remember it whilst he was preaching.

> Lord, make me from this hour
> Thy loving child to be,
> Kept by Thy power,
> Kept by Thy power,
> From all that grieveth Thee.

And the clergyman's text was in Colossians 1 : 12, "Meet to be partakers of the inheritance". He repeated it very slowly, and Christie whispered it softly to himself, that he might be able to teach it to old Treffy.

"'Meet to be partakers of the inheritance.' What is the inheritance?" asked the clergyman. "My dear friends, our inheritance is that city bright of which we have been speaking so much, 'Home, sweet Home', our Father's home. We are not there yet, but for all Christ's washed ones there is a bright home above. Jesus is preparing it for us; it is our inheritance. Oh," said the clergyman, very earnestly, "I wonder how many in this room have a home up there. You may have a wretched, uncomfortable home on earth; is it your *only* home? Is there no home for you in the bright city; no home in heaven?

"You might all have a home there," said the clergyman, "if you would only come to the fountain, if you would only say from the bottom of your heart, 'Lord, wash me, and I shall be whiter than snow.'"

And Christie smiled when the clergyman said his little prayer, for he thought of the snowdrops. And the clergyman thought of them too.

Then Mr. Wilton went on to say that he wished to-night to speak to those who *had* come to Jesus; who *had* taken their sin to Him, and who *had* been washed in His blood.

"That's me and old Treffy," said Christie to himself.

"My dear friends," said the clergyman, "all of you have an inheritance; you are the sons of a King; there is a place in the kingdom waiting for you. Jesus is getting that place ready for you, and I want to show you to-night that you must be made ready for it, meet or fit for the inheritance. One day, the Prince of Wales will be the King of England. This kingdom is his inheritance. As soon as he was born he had a right to it. But he had been educated and trained with great care, that he may be meet for the inheritance, that he may be fit to enjoy it, and able to use it. If he had had no education, if he had been brought up in one of these dismal black courts, though he might have a perfect right to be king, still he would not be able to enjoy it, he would feel strange, uncomfortable, out of place.

"Just so," said the clergyman, "is it with our inheritance. As soon as we are born again we have a right to it, we become sons and daughters of the King of kings. But we need to be prepared and made meet for the inheritance. We must be made holy within; we must be trained and taught to hate sin and to love all that is pure and holy. And this is the work of God's Holy Spirit.

"Oh, my friends, will you not ask for the gift of the Holy Spirit to renew your heart? It will not be all done in a day. You came to Jesus to be washed from the stain of sin. He did that at once; He gave you at once the right to the inheritance. But you will not be made holy at once. Little by little, hour by hour, day by day, the Holy Spirit will make you more and more ready for the inheritance. You will become more and more like Jesus. You will hate sin more; you will love Jesus more; you will become more holy.

"But, oh! let no one think," said the clergyman, "that being good will ever give you a *right* to the inheritance. If I were to be ever so well educated, if I were to be taught a hundred times better than the Prince of Wales has been, it would never give me a right to be King of England. No, my friends, the only way in to 'Home, sweet Home', the only way to obtain a right to the inheritance, is by the blood of Jesus. There is no other way, no other right.

"But, after the dear Lord has given us the right to the kingdom, He always prepares us for it. A forgiven soul will always lead a holy life. A soul that has been washed white will always long to keep clear of sin. Is it not so with you? Just think of what Jesus has done for you? He has washed you in His blood; He has taken your sins away at the cost of His life. Will you do the very things that grieve Him? Will you be so ungrateful as to do that? Will you?

"Oh, surely not; surely you will say, in the words of the third verse of our hymn -

> Lord, make me from this hour
> Thy loving child to be,
> Kept by Thy power,
> Kept by Thy power,
> From all that grieveth Thee.

And surely you will ask Him very, very earnestly to give you that Holy Spirit, who alone can make you holy. And when the work is done," said the clergyman, "when you are made meet, made fit for the inheritance, the Lord will take you there. He will not keep you waiting. Some are made ready very quickly. Others have to wait long, weary years of discipline. But all the King's sons shall be ready at last, all shall be taken home, and shall enter upon the inheritance. Will *you* be there?"

And with that question the clergyman ended his sermon, and the little congregation broke up very quietly, and went home with thoughtful faces.

Christie lingered near the door till the clergyman came out. He asked very kindly of old Treffy, and then put a few questions to Christie about the sermon; for he had been afraid whilst he had been preaching that he had not made it so clear that a child might understand. But he was cheered to find that the leading truth of the sermon was impressed on little Christie's mind, and that he would be able to carry to old Treffy something at least, of what he had heard.

For Christie was taught of God, and into hearts prepared by the Holy Spirit the seed is sure to sink. The Lord has prepared them for the word, and prepared the word for them, and the sower has only to put his hand into his basket and scatter the seed prayerfully over the softened soil. It will sink in, spring up, and bring forth fruit.

The clergyman felt the truth of this as he walked home. And he remembered where it was written, "The preparation of the heart is from the Lord".

"That is a word for me, as well as for my hearers," he said to himself. "Lord, ever let Thy preparation go before my preaching."

9
Treffy Enters the City

"CHRISTIE, boy," said Treffy, that night, when Christie had told him all he could remember of the sermon, and had repeated to him the third verse of the hymn, "Christie, boy, the Lord will have to get *me* ready very fast, very fast indeed."

"Oh, maybe not, Master Treffy," said Christie, uneasily; "maybe not so fast as you think."

"The month's nearly up, Christie," said old Treffy; "and I think I'm getting very near the city, very near to 'Home, sweet Home'. I can almost see the letters over the gate sometimes, Christie."

But Christie could not answer. His face was buried in his hands, and his head sank lower and lower as he sat beside the fire. And, at length, though he tried to keep it in, there came a great sob, which reached old Treffy's heart. He put his hand lovingly on Christie's head, and for some time neither of them spoke. But when the heart is very sore silence often does more to comfort than words can do, only it must be the silence which comes from a full heart, not from an empty one. Treffy's old heart was very full of loving, yearning pity for poor little Christie.

"Christie, boy," he said at length, "you wouldn't keep me outside the gate, would you?"

"No, no, Master Treffy," said Christie, "not for the world I wouldn't; but I do wish I was going in too."

"It seems to me, Christie boy, the Lord has got some work for you to do for Him first. I'm a poor, useless old man, Christie, very tottering and feeble, so He's going to take me home, but you have all your life before you, Christie, boy, haven't you?"

"Yes," said Christie, with a sigh, for he was thinking what a long, long time it would be before he was as old as Master Treffy, and before the golden gates would be opened to him.

"Wouldn't you *like* to do something for Him, Christie boy," said old Treffy, "just to show you love Him?"

"Ay, Master Treffy, I should," said Christie, in a whisper.

"Christie, boy," said old Treffy, suddenly raising himself in bed, "I would give all I have; yes, *all*, Christie, even my old organ, and you know how I've loved her, Christie, but I'd give her up, her and everything else, to have one year of my life back again - one year - to show Him that I love Him. Just to think," he said regretfully, "that He gave His life for me, and died ever such a dreadful death for me, and I've only got a poor little miserable week left to show that I love Him. Oh, Christie, boy! Oh, Christie, boy! It seems so ungrateful; I can't bear to think of it."

It was Christie's turn now to be the comforter.

"Master Treffy," he said, "just you tell the Lord that; I'm sure He'll understand."

Treffy clasped his hands at once, and said, earnestly -

"Lord Jesus, I do love Thee; I wish I could do something for Thee, but I've only another week to live - only another week; but oh, I do thank Thee; I would give anything to have some of my life back again, to show my love to Thee; please understand what I mean. Amen."

Then old Treffy turned over and fell asleep. Christie sat for some time longer by the fire. He had tried to forget how short a time he had with his old master, but it had all come back to him now. And his heart felt very sad and desolate. It is a very dreadful thing to lose the only friend you have in the world. And it is a very dreadful thing to see before you a thick, dark cloud, and to feel that it hangs over your pathway, and that you must pass through it. Poor Christie was very full of sorrow, for he 'feared as he entered into the cloud'. But Treffy's words came back to his mind, and he said, with a full heart -

"Lord Jesus, do help me to give my life to Thee. Oh, please help me to spare old Treffy! Amen."

Then, rather comforted, he went to bed.

The next morning he looked anxiously at old Treffy. He seemed weaker than usual, and Christie did not like to leave him. But they had very little money left, and Treffy seemed to wish him to go; so Christie went on his rounds with a heavy heart. He determined to go to the suburban road that he might tell little Mabel and her mother how much worse his dear old master was. It is such a comfort to speak of our sorrow to those who will care to hear.

Thus Christie stopped before the house with the pretty garden in front of it. The snowdrops were over now, but the primroses had taken their place, and the garden looked very gay and cheerful. But Christie had no heart to look at it; he was gazing up anxiously at the nursery window for little Mabel's face. But she was not to be seen, so he turned the handle of his organ and played *Home, sweet Home*, her favourite tune, to attract her attention. A minute after he began to play he saw little Mabel coming quickly out of the house and running towards him. She did not smile at him as usual, and she looked as if she had been crying, Christie thought.

"Oh, organ-boy," she said, "don't play to-day. Mamma is ill in bed, and it makes her head ache."

Christie stopped at once; he was just in the midst of the chorus of *Home, sweet Home*, and the organ gave a melancholy wail as he suddenly brought it to a conclusion.

"I am so sorry, missie," he said.

Mabel stood before him in silence for a minute or two, and Christie looked down upon her, very pitifully and tenderly.

"Is she very bad, missie?" he said.

"Yes," said little Mabel, "I think she must be: Papa looks so grave, and nurse won't let us play; and I heard her tell Cook that Mother would never be any better," she added, with a little sob, which came from the bottom of her tiny heart.

"Poor little missie!" said Christie, sorrowfully; "poor little missie, don't fret so; oh, don't fret so!"

And as Christie stood looking down on the little girl a great tear rolled down her cheek and fell on her little white arm.

Mabel looked up suddenly.

"Christie," she said. "I think Mother must be going to 'Home, sweet Home', and I want to go too."

"So do I," said Christie, with a sigh, "but the gates won't open to me for a long, long time."

Then the nurse called Mabel in, and Christie walked sorrowfully away. The world seemed very full of trouble to him. Even the sky was overcast, and a cutting east wind chilled Christie through and through. The spring flowers were nipped by it, and the budding branches were sent backwards and forwards by each fresh gust of the wind, and Christie felt almost glad that it was so cheerless. He was very sad and unhappy, very restless and miserable. He had begun to wonder if God had forgotten him; the world seemed to him so wide and desolate. His old master was dying, his little friend Mable was in trouble, there seemed to be sorrow everywhere. There seemed to be no comfort for poor Christie.

Wearily he returned homewards, and dragged himself up the steep staircase to the attic. He heard a voice within, a low, gentle voice, the sound of which soothed Christie's ruffled soul. It was the clergyman, and he was reading to old Treffy.

Treffy was sitting up in bed, with a sweet smile on his face, eagerly listening to every word. And as Christie came in, the clergyman was reading this verse: "Peace I leave with you, My peace I give unto you; not as the world giveth, give I unto you. Let not your heart be troubled, neither let it be afraid."

"That's a sweet verse for you, Treffy," said the clergyman.

"Ay," said Treffy, brightening, "and for poor Christie too; he's very cast down, is Christie, sir."

"Christie," said the minister, laying his hand on his shoulder, "why is *your* heart troubled?"

But Christie could not answer. He turned suddenly away from the minister, and throwing himself on old Treffy's bed, he sobbed bitterly.

The clergyman's heart was very full of sympathy for poor Christie. He knelt down beside him, and putting his arm round him, with almost a mother's tenderness, he said gently -

"Christie, shall we go together to the Lord Jesus, and tell Him of your sorrow?"

And then, in very plain, simple words, which Christie's heart could understand, the clergyman asked the dear Lord to look on the poor lonely child, to comfort him and to bless him, and to make him feel that he had one Friend who would never go away. Long after the clergyman had gone, when the attic was quite still and Treffy was asleep, Christie heard, as it were, a voice in his heart, saying to him, "Let not your heart be troubled." Then he fell asleep in peace.

He was awakened by his old master's voice.

"Christie!" said Treffy; "Christie, boy!"

"Yes, Master Treffy," said Christie jumping up hastily.

"Where's the old organ, Christie? asked Treffy.

"She's here, Master Treffy," said Christie, "all right and safe."

"Turn her, Christie," said Treffy, "play *Home, sweet Home.*"

"It's the middle of the night, Master Treffy," said Christie; "folks will wonder what's the matter."

But Treffy made no answer, and Christie crept to his side with a light, and looked at his face. It was very altered and strange. Treffy's eyes were shut, and there was that in his face which Christie had never seen there before. He did not know what to do. He walked to the window and looked out. The sky was quite dark, but one bright star was shining through it and looking in at the attic window. "Let not your heart be troubled," it seemed to say to him. And Christie answered aloud, "Lord, dear Lord, help me."

As he turned from the window Treffy spoke again, and Christie caught the words, "Play, Christie, boy, play."

He hesitated no longer. Taking the organ from its place he turned the handle, and slowly and sadly the notes of *Home, sweet Home* were sounded forth in the dark attic. The old man opened his eyes as Christie played, and, when the tune was over, he called the boy to him, and drawing him down very close to him, he whispered -

"Christie, boy, the gates are opening now. I'm going in. Play again, Christie, boy."

It was hard work playing the three other tunes, they seemed so out of place in the room of death.

But Treffy did not seem to hear them. He was murmuring softly to himself the words of the prayer, "Wash me, and I shall be whiter than snow! Whiter than snow, whiter than snow."

And, as Christie was playing *Home, sweet Home* for the second time, old Treffy's weary feet passed within the gates. He was at home at last, in "Home, sweet Home".

And little Christie was left outside.

10
"No Place like Home"

THE next morning, some of the lodgers in the great room below remembered having heard sounds in the stillness of the night which had awakened them from their dreams and disturbed their slumbers. Some maintained it was only the wind howling in the chimney, but others felt sure it was music, and said that the old man in the attic must have been amusing himself with the organ at midnight.

"Not he," said the landlady, when she heard of it; "he'll never play it again: he's a dying man, by what the doctor says."

"Just you go and ask him if he wasn't turning his old organ in the middle of last night," said a man from the far corner of the room. "I'll bet you a shilling he was."

The landlady went upstairs to satisfy his curiosity, and rapped at the attic door. No one answered, so she opened it and went in. Christie was fast asleep, stretched upon the bed where his old master's body lay. The tears had dried on his cheeks, and he was resting his head on one of old Treffy's cold, withered hands. The landlady's face grew grave, and she instinctively shuddered in the presence of death.

Christie woke with a start, and looked up in her face with a bewildered expression. He could not remember at first what had happened. But in a moment it all came back to him, and he turned over and moaned.

The landlady was touched by the boy's sorrow, but she was a rough woman and knew little of the way of showing sympathy, and Christie was not sorry when she went downstairs and left him to himself. As soon as the house was quiet he brought a neighbour to attend to old Treffy's body, and then crept out to tell the clergyman.

Mr. Wilton felt very deeply for the desolate child. Once again he committed him to his loving Father, to the Friend who would never leave him nor forsake him. And when Christie was gone he again knelt down, and thanked God with a very full heart for having allowed him to be the poor weak instrument in bringing this soul to Himself. There would be one at least at the beautiful gates of "Home, sweet Home", watching for his home-going steps. Old Treffy would be waiting for him there. Oh, how good God had been to him! It was with a thankful heart that he sat down to prepare his sermon for the next day, on the last verse of the hymn. And what he had just heard of old Treffy helped him much in the realization of the bright city of which he was to speak.

Mr. Wilton looked anxiously for Christie when he entered the crowded mission-room on Sunday evening. Yes, Christie was there, sitting as usual on the front bench, with a very pale and sorrowful face, and with heavy downcast eyes. And when the hymn was being sung the clergyman noticed that the tears were running down the boy's cheeks, though he rubbed them away with his sleeve as fast as they came. But Christie looked up almost with a smile when the clergyman gave out his text. It was from Revelation 7 : 14, 15: 'These are they which came out of great tribulation, and have washed their robes, and made them white in the blood of the Lamb. Therefore are they before the throne of God.'

"To-night," said the clergyman, "I am to speak of 'Home, sweet Home', and of those that dwell there, the great multitude of the redeemed. It is a very holy place, there is no speck on the golden pavement, no evil can be found within the city. The tempter can never enter there, sin is unknown; all is very, very holy. And on the white robes of those who dwell there there is no stain; pure and clean and spotless, bright and fair as light, are those robes of theirs. Nothing to soil them, nothing to spoil their beauty, they are made white for ever in the blood of the Lamb, therefore are they before the throne of God.'"

"Oh," said the clergyman, "never forget that this is the only way to stand before that throne! Being good will never take you there, not being as bad as others will avail you nothing; if you are ever to enter heaven, you must be washed white in the blood of the Lamb."

"St. John was allowed to look into heaven, and he saw a great company of these redeemed ones, and they were singing a new song, to the praise of Him who had redeemed them. And since St. John's time," said the clergyman, "oh, how many have joined their number! Every day, every hour, almost every moment, some soul stands before the city gates. And to every soul washed in the blood of Jesus those gates of pearl are thrown open; they are all dressed one by one in a robe of white, and as they walk through the golden streets, and stand before the throne of glory, they join in that song which never grows old - 'Amen. Blessing, and glory, and wisdom, and thanksgiving, and honour, and power, and might, be unto our God for ever and ever. Amen.'"

"And, my friends," said the clergyman, "as the holy God looks on these souls He sees in them no trace of sin, the blood has taken it all away; even in His sight they are all fair, there is no spot in them. They are faultless and stainless, perfectly pure and holy."

"Oh, my friends, will you ever join their number? This is a dark, dismal, dying world; will you be content never to enter 'Home, sweet Home'? Oh, will you delay coming to the fountain, and then wake up, and find you are shut out of the city bright, and that for ever?"

"One old man," said the clergyman, "to whom I was talking last week is now spending his first Sunday in that city bright."

A stillness passed over the room when the clergyman said this, and Christie whispered to himself, "He means Master Treffy. I know he does."

"He was a poor sin-stained old man," the clergyman went on, "but he took Jesus at His word, he came to the blood of Christ to be washed, and even here he was made whiter than snow. And two nights ago the dear Lord sent for the old-man, and took him home. There was no sin-mark found on his soul, so the gates were opened to him, and now in the snowy dress of Christ's redeemed he stands, 'faultless and stainless, faultless and stainless, safe in that happy home.'"

"If I were to hear next Sunday," said the clergyman, "that any one of you was dead, could I say the same of you? Whilst we are meeting here, would you be in 'Home, sweet Home'? Are you indeed washed in the precious blood of Christ? Have you indeed been forgiven? Have you indeed come to Jesus?"

"Oh, do answer this question in your own heart!" said Mr. Wilton, in a very earnest voice. "I do want to meet every one of you in 'Home, sweet Home'. I think that when God takes me there I shall be looking out for all of you, and oh, how I trust we shall all meet there - all meet at home!"

"I cannot say more to-night," said the minister, "but my heart is very full; God grant that each one of you may now be washed in the blood of Jesus, and even in this life be made whiter than snow, and then say with a grateful heart, 'Lord, I will work for Thee, love Thee, serve Thee all I can' -

Till in the snowy dress
Of Thy redeemed I stand,
Faultless and stainless,
Faultless and stainless,
Safe in that happy land!"

And then the service was over, and the congregation went away. But Christie never moved from the bench on which he was sitting. His face was buried in his hands, and he never looked up, even when the clergyman laid his hand kindly on his shoulder.

"Oh," he sobbed at last, "I want to go home; my mother's gone, and old Treffy's gone, and I want to go, too!"

The clergyman took Christie's little brown hand in both of his, and said, "Christie, poor little Christie, the Lord does not like to keep you outside the gate; but He has work for you to do a little longer, and then the gates will be opened, and home will be all the sweeter after the dark time down here." And then with other gentle and loving words he comforted the child, and then once more he prayed with him, and Christie went away with a lighter heart. But he could not help thinking of the last Sunday evening, when he had hastened home to tell Treffy about the third verse of the hymn.

There was no one to-night to whom Christie could tell what he had heard. He waited a minute outside the attic door as if he were almost afraid to go in, but it was only for a minute, and when he walked in all fear passed away.

The sun was setting, and some rays of glory were falling on old Treffy's face as he lay on the bed. They seemed to Christie as if they came straight from the golden city, there was something so bright and so unearthly about them. And Christie fancied that Treffy smiled as he lay on the bed. It might be fancy, but he liked to think it was so.

And then he went to the attic window and looked out. He almost saw the golden city, far away amongst those wonderous bright clouds. It was a strange, glad thought, to think that Treffy was there. What a change for him from the dark attic! Oh, how bright heaven would seem to his old master!

Christie would have given anything just to see for one minute what Treffy was doing. "I wonder if he will tell Jesus about me, and how I want to come home," said Christie to himself.

And as the sunset faded away and the light grew less and less, Christie knelt down in the twilight, and said from the bottom of his heart -

"O Lord, please make me patient, and please some day take me to live with Thee and old Treffy in 'Home, sweet Home'."

11
Alone in the World

LITTLE Christie was the only mourner who followed old Treffy to the grave. It was a poor parish funeral. Treffy's body was put into a parish coffin, and carried to the grave in a parish hearse. But, oh, it did not matter, for Treffy was at home in 'Home, sweet Home'; all his sorrows and troubles were over, his poverty was at an end, and in 'the Father's house' he was being well cared for.

But the man who drove the hearse was not inclined to lose time upon the road, and Christie had to walk very quickly, and sometimes almost to run, to keep up with him; and on their way they passed another and a very different funeral. It was going very slowly indeed. There was a large hearse in front, and six funeral carriages, filled with people, followed. And as Christie passed close by them in the middle of the road he could see that the mourners within looked very sorrowful, and as if they had been crying very much. But in one carriage he saw something which he never forgot. With her head resting on her papa's shoulder, and her little white sorrowful face pressed close to the window, was his little friend Mabel.

"So her mother is dead," said Christie to himself, "and this is her funeral! Oh, dear, what a very sad world this is!"

He was not sure whether Mabel had seen him, but the little girl's sorrow had sunk very deep into Christie's soul, and it was with a heavier heart than before that he hastened forward to overtake the hearse which was carrying his old master's body to the grave.

So the two funeral processions - that of the poor old man and that of the fair young mother - passed on to the cemetery, and over both bodies were pronounced the words, "Earth to earth, ashes to ashes, dust to dust". But all this time their happy souls were in 'Home, sweet Home', far, far away from the scene of sorrow. For a few days before, just at the same hour, two souls had left this world of woe, and had met together before the gates of pearl. And as they were both clean and white, both washed in the blood of the Lamb, the gates had been opened wide, and old Treffy and little Mabel's mother had entered the city together. And now they had both seen Jesus, the dear Lord whom they loved well, and in His presence they were even now enjoying fullness of joy.

Christie was obliged to give up the little attic after Treffy's death, for the landlady wished to let it for a higher rent. However, she gave the boy leave to sleep in the great lodging-room below, while she took possession of all Treffy's small stock of furniture in payment of the rent which he owed her.

But the organ was Christie's property; his old master had given it to him most solemnly about a week before he died. He had called Christie to his side, and told him to bring the organ with him. Then he had committed it to Christie's care.

"You'll take care of her, Christie," he had said, "and you'll never part with her, for my sake. And when you play *Home, sweet Home*, Christie, boy, you must think of me and your mother, and how we've both got there."

It was hard work for Christie the first day that he took out the organ after old Treffy's funeral; he did not so much mind playing *Rule Britannia*, or the *Old Hundredth*, or *Poor Mary Ann*, but when he came for the first time to *Home, sweet Home*, such a rush of feeling came over him that he stopped short in the middle and moved on without finishing it. The passers-by were surprised at the sudden pause in the tune, and still more so at the tears which were running down Christie's cheeks.

They little thought that the last time he had played that tune had been in the room of death, and that whilst he was playing it his dearest friend on earth had passed away into the true

'Home, sweet Home'. But Christie knew, and the notes of the tune brought back the recollection of that midnight hour. And he could not make up his mind to go on playing till he had looked up into the blue sky and asked for help to rejoice in old Treffy's joy. And then the chorus came very sweetly to him, "Home, sweet home; there's no place like home, there's no place like home. . ."

"And old Treffy's there at last," said Christie to himself as he finished playing.

One day, about a week after Treffy's funeral, Christie went up the suburban road in the hopes of seeing poor little Miss Mabel once more. He had never forgotten her sorrowful little face at the window of the funeral coach. And when we are in sorrow ourselves it does us good to see and sympathise with those who are in sorrow also. Christie felt it would be a great comfort to him to see the little girl. He wanted to hear all about her mother, and when it was that she had gone to "Home, sweet Home."

But when Christie reached the house he stood still in astonishment. The pretty garden was there just as usual, a bed of heartsease was blooming in the sunshine, and the stocks and forget-me-nots were in full flower. But the house looked very deserted and strange; the shutters of the lower rooms were up, and the bedrooms had no blinds in the windows, and looked empty and forlorn. And in the nursery window, instead of little Mabel's and Charlie's merry faces, there was a cross-looking old woman with her head bent down over her knitting.

What could be the matter? Where were the children gone? Surely no one else was lying dead in the house? Christie felt that he could not go home without finding out; he must ask the old woman. So he stood at the garden-gate, and turned the handle of the organ, hoping that she would look out and speak to him. But, beyond a passing glance, she gave no sign that she even heard it, but went on diligently with her work.

At length Christie could wait no longer; so stopping suddenly in the middle of *Poor Mary Ann*, he walked up the gravel path and rang the bell. Then the old woman put her head out of the window and asked what he wanted. Christie did not quite know what to say, so he came out at once with the great fear which was haunting him.

"Please, ma'am, is anyone dead?" he asked.

"Dead? No!" said the old woman, quickly. "What do you want to know for?"

"Please, could I speak to little Miss Mabel?" said Christie, timidly.

"No, bless you," said the old woman, "not unless you'd like a walk across the sea; she's in France by now."

"In France!" repeated Christie, with a bewildered air.

"Yes," said the old woman, "they've all gone abroad for the summer;" and then she shut the window in a decided manner, as much as to say, "And that's all I shall tell you about it."

Christie stood for a few minutes in the pretty garden before he moved away. He was very disappointed; he had so hoped to have seen his little friends, and now they were gone. They were far away in France. That was a long way off, Christie felt sure, and perhaps he would never see them again.

He walked slowly down the dusty road. He felt very lonely this afternoon, very lonely and forsaken. His mother was gone; old Treffy was gone; the lady was gone; and now the children were gone also! He had no one to cheer him or to comfort him; so he dragged the old organ wearily down the hot streets. He had not heart enough to play, he was very tired and worn out; yet he knew not where to go to rest. He had not even the old attic to call his home. But the pavement was so hot to his feet, and the sun was so scorching, that Christie determined to return to the dismal court, and to try to find a quiet corner in the great lodging-room.

But when he opened the door he was greeted by a cloud of dust; and the landlady called out to him to take himself off, she could not do with him loitering about at that time of day. So

Christie turned out again, very heart-sore and disconsolate; and going into a quiet street, he sheltered for some time from the hot sun, under a high wall which made a little shadow across the pavement.

Christie was almost too hot and tired even to be unhappy, and yet every now and then he shivered, and crept into the sunshine to be warmed again. He had a strange, sharp pain in his head, which made him feel very bewildered and uncomfortable. He did not know what was the matter with him, and sometimes he got up and tried to play for a little time, but he was so sick and dizzy that he was obliged to give it up, and to lie quite still under the wall, with the organ beside him, till the sun began to set. Then he dragged himself and his organ back to the large lodging-room. The landlady had finished her cleaning and was preparing the supper for her lodgers. She threw Christie a crust of bread as he came in, but he was not able to eat it. He crawled to a bench in the far corner of the room, and, putting his old organ against the wall beside him, he fell asleep.

When he awoke, the room was full of men; they were eating their supper and talking and laughing noisily. They took little notice of Christie, as he lay very still in the corner of the room. He could not sleep again, for the noise in the place was so great, and now and again he shuddered at the wicked words and coarse jests which fell on his ear almost every minute.

Christie's head was aching terribly, and he felt very, very ill; he had never been so ill in his life before. What would he not have given for a quiet little corner, in which he might have lain, out of the reach of the oaths and wickedness of the men in the great lodging-room! And then his thoughts wandered to old Treffy in 'Home, sweet Home'. What a different place his dear old master was in!

"There's no place like home, no place like home," said Christie to himself. "Oh, what a long way I am from 'Home, sweet Home'!"

12
Christie Well Cared For

"WHAT'S the matter with that little lad?" said one of the men to the landlady, as she was preparing their breakfast the next morning. "He's got a fever or something of the sort. He's been talking about one thing or another all night. I've had toothache, and scarcely closed my eyes, and he's never ceased chattering the night through."

"What did he talk about?" asked another man.

"Oh, all sorts of rubbish!" said the man with the toothache. "Bright cities, and funerals and snowdrops; and once he got up, and began to sing; I wonder you didn't hear him."

"It would have taken a great deal to make *me* hear him," said the other, "tired out as I was last night; what did he sing, though?"

"Oh, one of the tunes on his old organ! I expect he gets them in his head so that he can't get them out. I think it was *Home, sweet Home* he was trying last night;" and the man went to his work.

"Well, Mrs. White," said another man, "if the boy's in a fever, the sooner you get him out of this the better; we don't want all of us to take it."

When the men were gone the landlady went up to Christie to see if he were really ill. She tried to wake him, but he looked wildly in her face, and did not seem to know her. So she lifted him by main force into a little dark room under the stairs, which was filled with boxes and rubbish. She was not an unkind woman; she would not turn the poor child into the street in his present condition; so she made him up a little bed on the floor, and giving him a drink of water, she left him, to continue her work. That evening she fetched the parish doctor to see him, and he told her that Christie was in a fever.

For many days little Christie hung between life and death. He was quite unconscious of all that went on; he never heard the landlady come into the room; he never saw her go out. She was the only person who came near him, and she could give him very little attention, for she had so much to do. But she used to wonder why Christie talked so often of 'Home, sweet Home'; through all his wanderings of mind this one idea seemed to run. Even in his delirium, Christie was longing for the city bright.

But, after a time, Christie began to recover; he regained his consciousness, and slowly, very slowly, the fever left him. But he was so weak that he could not even turn in bed; and he could scarcely speak above a whisper. Oh, how long and dreary the days were to him! Mrs. White had begun to grow tired of waiting on him, and so Christie was for many a long hour without seeing anyone to whom he could speak.

It was a very dark little chamber, only lit from the passage, and Christie could not even see a bit of blue sky. He felt very much alone in the world. All day long there was no sound but the distant shouts of the children in the court; and in the evening he could hear the noise of the men in the great lodging-room. Often he was awake the greater part of the night, and lay listening to the ticking of the clock on the stairs, and counting the strokes hour after hour. And then he would watch the faint grey light creeping into the dark room, and listen to the footsteps of the men going out to their daily work.

No one came to see Christie. He wondered that Mr. Wilton did not ask after him, when he missed him from the mission-room. Oh, how glad Christie would have been to see him! But the days passed slowly by, and he never came, and Christie wondered more and more. Once he asked Mrs. White to fetch him to see him, but she said she could not trouble to go so far.

If little Christie had not had a friend in Jesus, his little heart would almost have broken, in the loneliness and desolation of those days of weakness. But though his faith was sometimes feeble, and he was then very downcast in spirit, yet at other times little Christie would talk with Jesus, as with a dear friend; in this way he was comforted. And the words which the clergyman had read to his old master were ever ringing in his ears, "Let not your heart be troubled."

Still those weeks did seem very long and tedious. At last he was able to sit up in bed, but he felt faint and dizzy whenever he moved. For he had had a very severe attack of fever, and he needed all manner of nourishing things to bring back his strength. But there was no one to attend to the wants of the poor motherless boy. No one, except the dear Lord; He had not forgotten him.

It was a close, tiring afternoon. Christie was lying upon his bed, panting with the heat, and longing for a breath of air. He was faint and weary, and felt very cast down and dispirited. "Please, dear Lord," he said aloud, "send someone to see me."

And even as he spoke the door opened, and the clergyman came in. It was too much for little Christie! He held out his arms to him in joy, and then burst into tears.

"Why, Christie," said the clergyman, "are you not glad to see me?"

"Oh," said little Christie, "I thought you were never coming, and I felt such a long way from home! Oh, I am so glad to see you!"

Then Mr. Wilton told Christie that he had been away from home, and that another clergyman had been taking his duty. But the night before he had preached for the first time since his return in the little mission-room, and he had missed Christie from the front bench. He had asked the woman who cleaned the room about him, and she had told him that Christie had never been there since he went away. The clergyman had wondered what was the matter, and had come as soon as he could to hear.

"And now, Christie," he said, "tell me all about these long, weary weeks."

But Christie was so glad and so happy now, that the past seemed like a long, troubled dream. He had woken up now, and had forgotten his sorrow and loneliness.

The clergyman and Christie had much pleasant talk together, and then Mr. Wilton said -

"Christie, I have had a letter about you, which I will read to you."

The letter was from little Mabel's papa, who was a friend of the clergyman.

MY DEAR MR. WILTON,

There is a poor boy of the name of Christie (what his surname is I do not know) living in a lodging-house in Ivy Court, Percy Street. He lived formerly with an old organ-grinder, but I believe the old man was thought to be dying some weeks ago. My dear wife took a great fancy to the boy, and my little Mabel frequently talks of him. I imagine he must be left in a very destitute condition; and I should be much obliged if you could find him out and provide for him some comfortable home with any respectable person who will act as a mother to him.

I enclose a cheque which will pay his expenses for the present. I should like him to go to school for a year or two, and then I intend, if the boy desires to serve Christ, to bring him up to work as a Scripture-reader amongst the lowest class of the people in your neighbourhood.

I think I could not perpetuate my dear wife's memory in any better way than by carrying out what I know were her wishes with regard to little Christie. No money or pains will I spare to do for him what she herself would have done, had her life been spared.

Kindly excuse me for troubling you with this matter; but I do not wish to defer it until our return, lest I lose sight of the boy. The dismal attic where Christie and his old master lived was the last place my dear wife visited before her illness; and I feel that the charge of this boy is a sacred duty which I must perform for her dear sake, and also for the sake of Him who has said, "Inasmuch as ye have done it unto one of the least of these My brethren, ye have done it unto Me."

Believe me, dear Mr. Wilton,
Yours very sincerely,
GERALD LINDSAY

"Christie," said the clergyman, "the dear Lord has been very good to you."

"Yes," said little Christie, "old Treffy was right; wasn't he, sir?"

"What did old Treffy say?" asked the clergyman.

"He said the Lord had some work for me to do for Him," said Christie, "and I didn't think there was anything I could do; but He's going to let me after all."

"Yes," said the clergyman, smiling; "shall we thank Him, Christie?"

So he knelt down by Christie's bed, and little Christie clasped his thin hands and added his words of praise -

"O Jesus I thank Thee so much for letting me have some work to do for Thee; and, please, I will stay outside the gates a little longer, to do something to show Thee how I love Thee. Amen."

"Yes, Christie," said the clergyman, as he rose to go, "you must work with a very loving heart. And when the work is over will come the *rest*. After the long waiting will come 'Home, sweet Home'."

"Yes," said Christie, brightly, "'there's no place like home, no place like home.'"

13
Christie's Work for the Master

IT was a hot summer's afternoon, some years after, and the air in Ivy Court was as close and stifling as it had been in the days when Christie and old Treffy lived there. Crowds of children might still be seen playing there, screaming and quarrelling, just as they had done then. The air was as full of smoke and dust and the court looked as desolate as it had done in those years gone by. It was still a very dismal and a very forlorn place.

So Christie thought, as he entered it that sultry day; it seemed to him as far as ever from 'Home, sweet Home'. Yet, of all the places which he visited as a Scripture-reader, there was no place in which Christie took such an interest as Ivy Court. For he could not forget those dreary days when he had been a little homeless wanderer, and had gone there for a night's lodging. And he could not forget the old attic, which had been the first place, since his mother's death, that he had been able to call home. It was to this very attic that he was going this afternoon. He climbed the rickety stairs, and as he did so he thought of the night when he had crept up them for the first time and had knelt down outside old Treffy's door, listening to the organ. Christie had never parted with that organ, his old master's last gift to him. And scarcely a week passed that he did not turn the handle and listen to the dear old tunes. And he always finished with *Home, sweet Home*, for he still loved that tune the best. And when Miss Mabel came to see him she always wanted to turn the old organ in remembrance of her childish days. She was not Miss Mabel any longer now, though Christie still sometimes called her so when they were talking together of the old days and of Treffy and his organ. But Mabel was married now to the clergyman under whom Christie was working, and she took great interest in the young Scripture-reader, and was always ready to help him with her advice and sympathy. And she would ask Christie about the poor people he visited, and he would tell her which of them most needed her aid. And where she was most needed young Mrs. Villiers was always ready to go.

And so it came to pass that when Christie knocked at the old attic door it was opened for him by Mrs. Villiers herself, who had just come there to see a poor sick woman. She had not met Christie in that attic since the days when they were both children, and Mabel smiled as he came in, and said to him, "Do you remember the occasion when we met here before?"

"Yes," said Christie, "I remember it well: there were four of us here then, Mrs. Villiers, and two out of the four have gone to the bright city which we talked of then."

"Yes," said Mabel, with tears in her eyes; "they are waiting for us in 'Home, sweet Home'."

The attic did not look any more cheerful that day than it had done when old Treffy lived there. The window panes were nearly all broken and filled with pieces of brown paper or rag. The floor was more rotten than ever and the boards seemed as if they must give way when Christie crossed the room to speak to a forlorn-looking woman who was sitting on a chair by the smouldering fire. She was evidently very ill and very unhappy. Four little children were playing about and making so much noise that Christie could hardly hear their mother speak when she told him she was "No better, no better at all," and she did not think she ever should be.

"Have you done what I asked you, Mrs. Wilson?" said Christie.

"Yes, sir, I've said it again and again, and the more I say it the more miserable it makes me."

"What is it, Christie?" said Mrs. Villiers.

"It's a little prayer, ma'am, I asked her to say: 'O God, give me Thy Holy Spirit, to show me what I am.'"

"And I think He has shown me," said the poor woman, sadly; "anyhow, I never knew I was such a sinner; and every day as I sit here by my fire I think it all over, and every night as I lie awake on my bed I think of it again."

"I've brought another prayer for you to say now, Mrs. Wilson," said Christie, "and I've written it out on a card, that you may be able to learn it quickly: 'O God, give me Thy Holy Spirit, to show me what Jesus is.' God has heard and answered your first prayer, so you may be sure He will hear this one also. And if he only shows you what Jesus is, I am sure you will be happy, for Jesus will forgive you your sin, and take away all its heavy burden."

The poor woman read the prayer aloud several times, and then Mrs. Villiers took a book from her pocket and began to read. It was a little much-worn Testament. It had once been blue, but, from constant use, the colour had faded, and the gilt edges were no longer bright. It was not the first time that same Testament had been in that old attic. For it was the same book from which Mabel's mother had read to old Treffy fifteen years before. How Mabel loved that book! Here and there was a pencil-mark which her mother had made against some favourite text, and these texts Mabel read again and again, till they became her favourites also. It was one of these which she read to the poor woman to-day: "The Blood of Jesus Christ, His Son, cleanseth us from all sin." And then Mrs. Villiers explained how ready Jesus is to save any soul that comes to Him, and how His blood is quite sufficient to take away sin.

The sick woman listened eagerly, and a tear came into Christie's eye as he said: "There is no text that I love like that, Mrs. Villiers. Mr. Wilton preached on it in the mission-room the second time I went there, and I felt as if I could sing for joy when I heard it; I well remember how I ran up the stairs of this attic, to tell it to my old master."

"And you've found it true, Christie?"

"Yes, ma'am, indeed I have, and Treffy found it true, too."

82

Then Mrs. Villiers and Christie took their leave; but as they were going down the steep staircase Christie said, "Have you time to call on Mrs. White for a few minutes, ma'am? She would be so glad to see you, and I don't think she will live very long."

Mrs. Villiers gladly agreed to go; so Christie knocked at the door at the bottom of the stairs. A young woman opened it, and they went in.

Mrs. White was lying on a bed in the corner of the room, and seemed to be asleep; but presently she opened her eyes, and when she saw Christie her face brightened, and she held out her hands in welcome. She was an old woman now and had given up taking lodgers several years before.

"Oh, Christie," she said. "I *am* glad to see you; I have been counting the hours till you came."

"Mrs. Villiers has come to see you to-day, Mrs. White."

"Oh, how good of you!" said the poor woman; "Christie said you would come some day."

"You have known Christie a long time, have you not?" asked Mrs. Villiers.

"Yes," said the old woman, "he came to me first as a little ragged boy, shivering with cold; and I liked the look of him, ma'am, he was so much quieter than some that came here; and I used to give him a crust sometimes, when he looked more starved than usual."

"Yes, Mrs. White," said Christie, "you were often very good to me."

"Oh, not as I should have been, Christie; they were only crusts I gave you, bits that were left from the men's meals, and not so much of them either; but you've come to me, and you've brought me the Bread of Life - not just bits and leavings, but enough and to spare, as much as I like, and more than enough for all I want."

"Oh, Christie," said Mrs. Villiers, "I am glad to hear this; the dear Lord has been very good to you; your work has not been in vain."

"In vain!" said the old woman. "I should think not! There's many a one, Mrs. Villiers, that will bless God in the home above for what you and your father have done for this lad; and there is no one who will bless Him more than I shall. I was as dark as a heathen till Christie came to me, and read to me out of his Bible, and talked to me of Jesus, and put it all so clear to me. And now I know that my sins are forgiven, and very soon the Lord will take me home; and - oh dear! - how nice that will be,

> Till in the snowy dress
> Of Thy redeemed I stand,
> Faultless and stainless,
> Faultless and stainless,
> Safe in that happy land!"

"I see that Mrs. White knows your hymn, Christie," said Mrs. Villiers.

"Yes," said Christie, "I taught her it a long time ago, and she is as fond of it as my old master was."

After a little more conversation Mrs. Villiers took her leave, and Christie continued his round of visits. All that long, sultry afternoon he toiled on, climbing dark staircases, going down into damp cellars, visiting crowded lodging-houses; and everywhere, as he went, dropping seeds of the Word of life, sweet words from the Book of books, suited to the hearts of those with whom he met.

For in that Book Christie found there was a word for every need, and a message for every soul. There was peace for the sin-burdened, comfort for the sorrowful, rest for the weary, counsel for the perplexed, and hope for the dying. And Christie always prayed before he went out that God's Holy Spirit would give him the right word for each one whom he went to see. And, as he knocked at the door of a house, he always lifted up his heart in a silent prayer, something like this -

"Thou, Lord, who knowest the hearts of all men, give me the opportunity of saying something for Thee, and please help me to use it, and show me how to say the right word."

And so it was no wonder that God blessed him. It was no wonder that wherever he went Christie not only found opportunities of doing good, but was able to use these opportunities to the best advantage. It was no wonder that when the people were ill they always sent for the young Scripture-reader to read and pray with them. It was no wonder that the little children loved him, or that the poor, tired mothers were glad to sit down for a few minutes to hear him read words of comfort from the Book of Life. It was no wonder that all day long Christie found work to do for the Master and souls waiting to receive the Master's message. He was generally very tired when he went home at night, but he did not mind this. For he never forgot old Treffy's sorrow, a few days before he died, because he had only a week left in which to show his love to his Saviour. And Christie thanked God every day that He had given to him the honour and privilege of working for Him.

Christie lodged in a quiet street not far from Ivy Court. He used to live some way out of the town, for he liked to have a walk after his day's work was done; but he found that the poor people often wanted him for different things in the evening and at other times, and so he removed nearer to them and nearer to his work. And very often they would come to him with their troubles, and sit in his little room pouring out their grief. The young men especially were very glad to come to Christie's lodging to have a talk with him; and once a week Christie had a little prayer-meeting there, to which many of them came. And they found it a great help on their way to heaven.

When Christie opened the door of his lodging on the day of which I am writing, he heard a sound which very much surprised him. It was the sound of his old barrel-organ, and it was playing a few notes of *Home, sweet Home*. He wondered much who could be turning it, for he had forbidden the landlady's children to touch it, except when he was present to see that no harm came to it. He sometimes smiled to himself at his care over the old organ. It reminded him of the days when he had first played it, with old Treffy standing by him and looking over his shoulder, saying in an anxious voice, "Turn her gently, Christie, boy; turn her gently."

And now he was almost as careful of it as Treffy himself, and he would not on any account have it injured. And so he hastened upstairs to see who it could be that was turning it this morning. On his way he met his landlady, who said that a gentleman was waiting for him in his parlour, who seemed very anxious to see him, and had been sitting there for some time. And, when Christie opened the door, who should be turning the barrel-organ but his old friend Mr. Wilton.

They had not met for many years, for Mr. Wilton had settled in another part of England, where he had been preaching the same truths as he once preached in the little mission-room. But he had come to spend a Sunday in the scene of his former labours, and he was very anxious to know how his friend Christie was getting on, and whether he was still working for the Saviour and still looking forward to 'Home, sweet Home'.

It was a very affectionate meeting between Mr. Wilton and his young friend. They had much to talk about, not having seen each other for so long.

"So you still have the old organ, Christie," said Mr. Wilton, looking down at the faded silk, which was even more colourless than it had been in Treffy's days.

"Yes, sir," said Christie, "I could never part with it; I promised my old master that I never would, and it was his dying gift to me. And now often when I hear the notes of *Home, sweet Home*, it takes my thoughts to old Treffy, and I think what a happy time he must have had in 'the city bright' all these fifteen years."

"Do you remember how you used to want to go there, too, Christie?"

"Yes, Mr. Wilton, and I don't want it any the less now; but still I should like to live some years longer, if it is His will. There is so much to do in the world, isn't there, sir? And what I do only seems to me like a drop in the ocean when I look at the hundreds of people there are in these crowded courts. I could almost cry sometimes when I feel how little I can teach them."

"Yes, Christie," said Mr. Wilton, "there is a great deal to do, and we cannot do a tenth part, nor yet a thousandth part, of what there is to do; what we must strive after is, that the dear Master may be able to say to each of us, 'He hath done what he *could*.'"

Then Mr. Wilton and Christie knelt down and prayed that God would give Christie a blessing on his work, and would enable him to lead many of the people, in the courts and lanes of that wretched neighbourhood, to come to Jesus, that they might find a home in that city where Treffy was gone before.

14
"Home, Sweet Home" at Last

IT was Sunday evening, and Christie was once more in the little mission-room; but not now as a poor ragged boy, sitting on the front bench, and in danger of being turned out by the woman who lighted the gas-lamps. She would not dream of turning Christie out now, for the young Scripture-reader was a well-known man in the district. He was always there early, before any of the people arrived, and he used to stand at the door and welcome each one as they came in, helping the old men and women in their seats, and looking out anxiously for those whom he had invited for the first time during the week. And if any little ragged boys stole in, and seemed inclined to listen, Christie took special care of them, for he had not forgotten the day when he had first come to that very room, longing to hear a word of comfort to tell to his old master.

Mr. Wilton was to take the service that night, and Christie had been busy all afternoon giving special invitations to the people to be present, for he wanted them very much to hear his dear friend.

The mission-room was quite full when Mr. Wilton entered it. How it rejoiced him to see Christie going about amongst the people, with a kind word for each, and handing them the small hymn-books from which they were to sing!

"Come, for all things are now ready." That was Mr. Wilton's text. How still the mission-room was, and how earnestly all the people listened to the sermon! The clergyman first spoke of the marriage feast in the parable; so carefully spread, so kindly prepared, all ready there - and yet no one would come! There were excuses on all sides, every one was too busy or too idle to attend to the invitation; no one was ready to obey that gracious "Come".

And then Mr. Wilton spoke of Jesus, and how He had made all things ready for us; how pardon is ready and peace is ready; the Father's arms ready to receive us; the Father's love ready to welcome us; a home in heaven ready prepared for us. That, he said, was God's part of the matter.

"And what, my dear friends," he went on, "is *our* part? *Come*; 'come, for all things are now ready.' *Come*; you have only to come and take; you have only to receive this love. Come sin-stained soul; come, weary one; 'come, for all things are now ready.' *Now* ready. There is a great deal in that word *now*. It means to-night - this very Sunday; not next year, or next week; not to-morrow, but now - all things are *now* ready. God has done all He can, He can do no more, and He says to you, 'Come!' Will you not come? Are God's good things not worth having? Would you not like to lie down to sleep feeling that you were forgiven? Would you not like one day to sit down to the marriage supper of the Lamb?

"Oh, what a day that will be!" said Mr. Wilton, as he ended his sermon. "St. John caught a glimpse of its glory amidst the wonderful sights he was permitted to see. And so important was it, so good, so specially beautiful, that the angel seems to have stopped him, that St. John might write it down at once: Wait a minute, don't go any farther, take out your book and make a note of that - Write, 'Blessed are they which are called unto the marriage supper of the Lamb.'

"Are *you* one of those blessed ones?" asked the clergyman. "Are you washed in the blood of the Lamb? Will you sit down to that supper? Have you a right to enter into 'Home, sweet Home'? I know not what is your answer to these questions. But if you cannot answer me now, how will you in that day answer the great Searcher of hearts?"

And with this question the sermon ended, and the congregation left; those of them who had known Mr. Wilton still lingering behind, to shake hands with him, and to get a parting word of counsel or comfort.

Christie walked home by the clergyman's side.

"And now, Christie," said Mr. Wilton, "do you think you can be ready to start with me to-morrow morning at eight o'clock?"

"To start with you, sir?" repeated Christie.

"Yes, Christie; you have had hard work lately, and I have asked leave from Mr. Villiers to take you home with me, that you may have a little country air and quiet rest. I am sure it will not be lost time, Christie; you will have time for quiet reading and prayer, and you will be able to gain strength and freshness for future work. Well, do you think you can be ready in time?"

Christie thought there was no fear of his being late. He thanked Mr. Wilton with a voice full of feeling, for he had sometimes longed very much for a little pause in his busy life.

And the next day found Christie and Mr. Wilton rapidly travelling towards the quiet country village in which Mr. Wilton's church was to be found.

What was the result of that visit may be gathered from the following extract, taken from a letter written by Christie to Mr. Wilton some months later -

I promised you that I would let you know about our little home. It is, I think, one of the happiest to be found in this world. I shall always bless God that I came to your village, and met my dear little wife.

At last I have a 'Home, sweet Home' of my own. We are so happy together! When I come home from work I always see her watching for me, and she has everything ready. And the evenings we spend together are very quiet and peaceful. Nellie likes to hear about all my visits during the day, and the poor people are already so fond of her they come to her in all their troubles. And we find it such a comfort to be able to pray together for those in whom we are interested, and together to take them to the Saviour.

Our little home is so bright and cheerful! I wish you could have seen it on the evening on which we arrived. Mrs. Villiers had made all ready for us, and with her own hand had put on the tea-table a lovely bunch of snowdrops and dark myrtle leaves. And I need not tell you that they reminded me of those which she had given me when she was little Miss Mabel, and when she taught me that prayer which I have never forgotten. 'Wash me, and I shall be whiter than snow.'

And now, dear Mr. Wilton, you may think of Nellie and me as living together in love and happiness in the dear little earthly home, yet still looking forward to the eternal home above, our true, our best, our brightest "HOME, SWEET HOME!"

Christie's Old Organ

There is a ci - ty bright, Closed are its gates to sin; Nought that de - fil - eth, Nought that de - fil - eth, Can ev - er en - ter in.

Saviour, I come to Thee,
O Lamb of God, I pray,
  Cleanse me and save me,
  Cleanse me and save me,
Wash all my sins away.

Lord, make me from this hour
Thy loving child to be,
  Kept by Thy power,
  Kept by Thy power,
From all that grieveth Thee.

Till in the snowy dress
Of Thy redeemed I stand,
  Faultless and stainless,
  Faultless and stainless,
Safe in that happy land!